CURIOSITY KILLED THE WITCH

MIDLIFE CURSES
BOOK TWO

VICTORIA CRAWFORD

CHAPTER 1

To find this cure, you must begin from a place where the past is contained within an edifice. There is culture or knowledge groomed for instruction.

The final words of Lord Ravin replayed over and over in my mind, and I couldn't help the uncertainty that raged within me. We needed to solve this puzzle. It was the only way I could get a cure for Chloe. We also needed to imprison the Dark God in the underworld. No biggie, right? Just that no one had ever done it before or stayed alive long enough to tell the world how. I almost laughed at the folly. I could just imagine saying, "Hello everyone. I went down to the underworld and went toe to toe with a Dark God. He was powerful, but I imprisoned him. Yup, that was me." Sure, that was believable from the woman who couldn't perform a simple location spell without screwing it up. A death mission should be a walk in the park for a witch with faulty magic.

We all stood around the kitchen table. Linda had provided a fresh batch of cookies, which Sinn and I were happy to devour. I loved that she baked when she was working through problems. I bit my nails. Her routine seemed far healthier. I went to the counter, put a pot of water on the stove, and grabbed a box of mint tea from the cupboard.

"So, what are we going to do?" Linda asked, taking a bite of her cookie with her brown eyes fixed on me. The last thing I wanted to admit was I had reached my breaking point, but I was stumped on my next course of action. I flicked on the element, needing something I could control.

"You said we should do both, right?" I asked, angling my body to face them. Sinn's face had no expression, and I wondered if he had lost faith in our cause. Was he worried about our chances of success? He had originally wanted to trap the Dark God. Was he having reservations? What dilemma was he pondering? These questions kept popping into my brain, and my lack of answers soured my mood. My mind drifted to Chloe and how I had made her condition worse. If the Dark God was watching, he would be laughing at my foolishness and how I failed to listen to the warnings before giving Chloe the potion made by Elder Sabrina.

"We need to imprison this god and try to ensure that no family goes through this pain in the future. We owe humanity that," Linda said.

I huffed. "Humanity? Right now, my duty is to my daughter and how I can cure her. Humanity needs a savior, not a martyr. If we go to the underworld, we will be going through hell, literally. And for what? A slim chance that we might imprison a god that has done everything to ensure that we fail?" I snapped back.

Sinn glanced between us, but said nothing.

Linda rolled her eyes. "Sinn, you need to back me up here. Bree is reacting like a mother. I get that, but Chloe isn't the only issue. If we don't stop the Dark God, then Chloe won't have a world to live in. Help me bring her back to her senses," she said to Sinn.

He looked at me as my eyes narrowed on him. Daring him to agree with her. For a moment, we kept our gaze locked, but if he was telling me anything through his eyes, I wasn't getting it. Chloe was my first priority.

"Let's say we want to do both. How do we go about it? Surely, there is something two powerful witches can come up with. A spell or ritual that will help us," Sinn said, and I folded my arms again. This time, I shifted my gaze to Linda, waiting for her to support Sinn's suggestion.

"If we want to do anything, I think our best bet is the riddle left by Lord Ravin. I think if we solve it, we might figure out where to find the cure, and that would save Chloe," Linda said.

"What about the other problem? How do we go about it?" I asked, facing Sinn as he had a better understanding of the underworld and hoped he had an answer.

I grabbed the kettle when it began to boil and poured it into the teapot with the two tea bags. "In the scrolls, it was mentioned that the Dark God may already have a portal on earth. If this is true, that is the gateway to the underworld, our gateway to the underworld. But, to find this portal, we need to solve the riddle given by Lord Ravin. It is also the only clue we have, so that's our only option," Sinn said, and I nodded in agreement. All our answers revolved around solving the riddle, and I looked at the words again.

"To find this cure, you must begin from a place where the past is contained within an edifice. There is culture or knowledge groomed for instruction."

As I read aloud, a thought filled my mind, and I paused, looking at Linda and Sinn.

"What's the matter?" Linda asked, and I was silent for a second.

I grabbed three cups and poured the tea before passing

one to Sinn and then Linda. "I was just thinking. We have been planning to stop the Dark God. But isn't there a chance that this god wants to stop us too? What if he is plotting to thwart our plans? Does he know we are plotting against him?"

Sinn took a sip of tea before clearing his throat. He was the only person with some knowledge of the Dark God, and we needed answers.

"Always assume that the Dark God can see you. He has the power to see things that are of importance to him. He might be watching us and we can't block his sight if he chooses to observe us. We can only plan ahead and for as many unforeseen contingencies as possible. He will try to stop us, but if our will is strong, and the gods favor us, we should be able to imprison him," Sinn said, but it didn't feel like an assurance of our safety. There was no easy way to talk about death, and I feared ours would be imminent as soon as we stepped into the underworld.

"Let's talk about the riddle. How do we solve it?" Linda asked, pulling my mind from the dark thoughts. Sinn nodded, agreeing with her. Before I could say anything else, he took a sheet of paper and rewrote the riddle boldly on it, setting the paper in front of us.

To find this cure, you must begin from a place where the past is contained within an edifice. There is culture or knowledge groomed for instruction.

"To find this cure, you must begin from a place where the past is contained within an edifice. What does that even mean?" Linda asked, and I chuckled. I held my teacup as I moved back to the table, focusing my gaze on the mystery words before me.

"It means we are looking for a place, an edifice," Sinn replied, and I rolled my eyes.

"That is the most obvious explanation. There must be another meaning embodied in the text. We can't just be looking for any type of place or building. There are specifics and we need to identify them," I said, slightly raising my voice. When I was done talking, I looked up to see both Sinn and Linda's eyes fixed on me. I was the only one looking at the words while they stared at me. It made me uncomfortable.

"What have I done this time?" I said, expecting that I had done something to offend them.

"Why are you on edge? I thought we were making progress." Linda asked, and my eyes widened. She was always a stickler for direct questioning. I looked to Sinn, who said nothing. It was obvious that he agreed with Linda. I was being bitchy.

"Edge? Me?" I said as they nodded.

"I don't know…" I trailed off. "I didn't realize I was on edge. I'm sorry. I guess the whole death thing got to me."

I met their gaze, but they didn't look too convinced. My excuse was flimsy, but it was the only one I could think of. I didn't blame them. They were just looking out for me and my daughter.

"This has become bigger than us. Bigger than Chloe's life. I guess I am reeling. Can we focus on solving this riddle again?" I asked, and they relaxed.

"Fair enough," Sinn said. We focused on the words before us.

"So, we know it is a building, an edifice. But what kind of edifice?" Linda asked, and we all leaned over the paper, hoping it would bring inspiration. The words swirled in my mind, yet I couldn't make sense of them.

"An edifice where the past is contained…" I trailed off again and thought about the meaning of that word.

Sinn frowned. "The past could mean anything. It could

mean stories of old. It could be a building of the old religion, or a place where darkness reigns. Anything." He looked at us hopefully, but no reply was forthcoming.

"But, in this case, the past must be something that could stand the test of time. Something that Lord Ravin knew would be prominent in this century and I sure as hell know that it isn't referring to the old religion, at least not yet," I said.

"What was happening in the ancient times that is still prominent right now?" Linda asked, and I began recalling my history. If we could understand what was prominent, then and still utilized in our century, it could go a long way in solving our riddle.

"Well, the ancient time was a time of magic, death, and war. Humans and witches wanted dominion over themselves, and this led to cities being conquered and towns looted. It was also a trend back then to keep things of value. Gold, silver, bronze, gems, art, and anything else rare," Sinn said casually, and it all clicked.

"That's it!" I said, taking the paper in my hands and smiling as Sinn and Linda came to my side.

"You have figured it out?" Linda asked, and I gave her a weak smile.

"I think I have."

"Where is it?" Sinn asked.

"We are missing the whole point of the riddle. It isn't just the place we should be focusing on. We should also focus on the last line of the riddle. We can't leave that out," I said, and Sinn frowned, still as confused as Linda.

"There is culture or knowledge groomed for instruction. What does that even mean?" Sinn asked, and I chuckled. My frustration had turned to fruition, and I was eager to share.

"A place where we can find the past, and it also has

culture or knowledge groomed for instruction. Where is the one place you can find cultural information and learn new things? In this place you rarely find things of our time, but many of the ancient times. Items begotten from war or donated in peace. Artifacts preserved for their cultural heritage." I asked, and they frowned for a second.

"Don't call me stupid, but I could swear that you just described a museum," Linda said weakly, taking a sip of her tea.

"Yesssss! A museum. This is the only connection we have with the past. It is also an edifice and when you visit the museum, you meet different cultures and gain knowledge about different ways of life. I think the answer to this riddle is a museum. We just have to figure out which museum," I said, smiling as my excitement grew. After the disaster with the potion, I needed this small victory.

"That's some genius-level reasoning," Sinn smirked at me as I finished and my cheeks flushed. Sinn and his comments. That man's smile was like sex on a stick, and he made it harder to concentrate on the task at hand.

"I wouldn't have come up with that without your help. That story of how life was back in the day helped a lot, and my riddle-solving skills would have been nonexistent if we didn't do it together. We have a long way to go. We still have to find out what museum the riddle is referring to."

"There is only one museum it could refer to. The one we all visited as kids when our parents were the top witches," Linda said.

I looked at Linda, and the confusion showed on my face. "There are four museums in Drima Falls. We have visited all of them. Which one are you talking about?"

"The only one our parents were also excited to visit. The Museum of Ancient Arts," she replied, and my childhood memories came back like a rushing wind. I recalled how my mother loved visiting the museum of Ancient Arts. She acted like every time was her first, and I wondered if she found the scrolls in one of her many visits.

"If the cure is at the Museum of Ancient Arts, we must find it and save Chloe," I said, looking at Sinn, who gave me a weak smile. I hated to admit that if the cure was really at the museum, it wasn't just going to be handed to us, and I wondered what we were going to face to acquire it.

CHAPTER 2

I would be damned if we got what we needed from the museum without a fight, especially with the possibility that the Dark God was watching our every move. I rinsed my teacup in the sink and put it on the drying rack. Then went to the front room and motioned for Sinn and Linda to follow. We had some decisions to make.

"It's going to take about an hour and a half to get to the Museum of Ancient Arts. So, what do we do from there?" Linda asked as I sat down on the couch. The whirlwind of papers had been cleaned, but the blinds were twisted, reminding me of the maelstrom I had created.

"Linda, as much as I want us to do this together, I need you here," I said as she frowned at me. Sinn put his cup in the sink and joined me on the couch. His thick thigh rubbed against mine, and I tried not to let the heat from his body affect me. What happened between us was a one-time thing, and I would keep telling myself that until I believed it. Ours was a partnership of convenience. I needed him, and he was magically attached to me.

"What do you mean? Why shouldn't I go with you?" She

asked. The hurt was evident in her voice. As much as it broke my heart, I couldn't let her go with me.

"I'm sorry, Linda. You can't come to the museum with us. It doesn't make sense to risk us all," I said as her frown deepened. I knew she was pissed, assuming this was like the high school incident. But I wouldn't put all my eggs in a basket. This was too important, even if it hurt her feelings.

"May I ask why?" Sinn asked, and I angled my body to face him. He had a stern look on his face, and I could tell he didn't agree with my decision.

"Yeah. Why wouldn't you want me to come with you?" Linda asked, and I hoped they would understand my reasoning. She took a seat in the opposite chair.

"Isn't it obvious? I can't let all three of us go to the Museum of Ancient Arts. First, there is Chloe. You know how sick she is and she can't take care of herself. We need to be there for her. If I'm going to the museum, you should stay with her. You know there is no one else I trust with her, Linda."

She sighed. "That's a dirty play. You know I love Chloe and will do anything to make her better."

"You don't need to tell me how much you love Chloe. I know you do. But your love for her isn't the only reason. You have magic, and I know you are strong enough to protect her from danger. If something goes wrong at the Museum, we need you here."

"She has never been attacked since she was cursed. Why would someone go after her now?" Linda asked. I didn't want to fight with her and needed her to understand my reasoning, but it seemed like I had failed to convince her, and Sinn wasn't helping my case.

"Have you not given any thought that she wasn't attacked because the Dark God knew the potion would be poison to her? Since there is a possibility that the Dark God is watching, then we must be careful about our choices. We need to protect Chloe because her death would remove our motivation to imprison the Dark God. Honestly, I would be devastated and wouldn't be able to carry on. Please, Linda," I pleaded, but Linda's face was devoid of emotions.

"Why can't Sinn stay? I mean, he is a demon and a demigod. He is strong enough to protect her," she said, and I couldn't hold it in anymore.

"Don't you get it, Linda? You are like a mother to Chloe, and you love her like a mother. If something happens to me, I need to know you are here for her. Sinn is here, and he is helping us, but his time in this world is finite. We have no idea how long that will be. He is as important as you are in this cause, but he can't be a mother to Chloe. Please, try to understand. We can't all go to the Museum of Ancient Arts. It might be dangerous. We could be walking into a trap. It's wise for one of us to stay behind, and you are the best candidate if things go south," I said, raising my voice slightly.

Sinn rubbed his leg. "She is right, Linda. We need you here. We might be walking into a trap. We need someone with reliable magic if things go bad and that someone is you," Sinn said, and a smile formed on my face. I had been waiting for him to back me up and I was almost giddy that he had. I winked at him and he returned a quick smile, revealing his white teeth. His smile brought memories of the time I was wrapped in his embrace. I thought about our last time together. As much as the coven warned me not to trust him and his kind, the words of Elder Sabrina played in my mind. I realized that I was trusting him more with every second we spent together, but his actions had spoken louder than words and he had died for me.

Linda stood and began pacing the living room. Then, she

crossed her arms, then rested her body against the wall as she said, "Fine, you win. I will stay with Chloe and protect her. But this means that whatever happens in the Museum of Ancient Arts, you'll have no witch backing you up. You will be alone with Sinn, and we don't know if he has any powers yet."

"Just because I haven't displayed my power doesn't mean I have none or that it's faulty," Sinn said, with his eyes on me. My eyes widened.

"Hey…" I trailed off. "That was a low blow, even for you, Sinn. So far, the only magic I have seen from you is sex appeal." I teased, and we all laughed.

Linda glanced at her wristwatch and then at us. "It's 10 A.M. If you need to rest or eat, you should do that now. You need to leave in two hours," she said in an orderly fashion, and I gave her a fake salute, drawing laughter from everyone again.

"Two hours is enough time to prepare for whatever the museum is going to throw at us," I said. I needed a shower, an hour of rest, and a good meal before hitting the road. Sinn needed the same, whether he admitted it or not.

I showered and made myself a peanut butter and jam sandwich. I changed into shorts and a t-shirt, then lay down for a quick nap. Sinn lay down beside me after his shower and my eyelids drooped as I inhaled his fresh masculine scent. I swore I never got to sleep before strong hands shook me.

"Hey, sleepyhead. It's time to go," Sinn called out and for a moment, I thought I was in a dream. His voice felt distant, and my eyes flew open when I felt his lingering touch on my shoulder.

"How long did I sleep for?" I asked, looking around my room. Linda was nowhere in sight. Sinn smiled at me and removed the strands of hair stuck in my face, tucking them behind my ears. Then, he pulled me into a sitting position and handed me a plate with toast on it, and pointed to a glass of milk on the side table for me.

My stomach growled, surprising me since I had just eaten. I smiled, angling my body to face Sinn as I asked, "how long did I sleep for, Sinn?" It was supposed to be a quick nap for an hour, but a part of me suspected it had been longer.

"The important thing is you are up and we can be on our way. Why do you want to know how long you slept?" He questioned, and I suspected when Sinn didn't want to answer, it was because he knew I might not like the outcome. This was one of those moments.

"Just tell me," I said, setting the plate on the bed beside me before returning my gaze to him. This time, I noticed that he had shaved his face. He was also wearing new clothes, ones that I hadn't seen before, and I was certain they were not one of Marcellus's outfits. It was new. Did he know his way around already? I asked myself, staring at him while lost in my thoughts.

"Fine. If you want to know. You went to bed a bit before 11 'o'clock and it is now 3 pm," he replied casually, taking a seat on the floral chair in my bedroom. My eyes widened as I did the math in my head.

"What? I slept for four hours? That's impossible. Don't we have somewhere to be?" I asked and jumped off the bed. Quickly, I rushed to my wardrobe, throwing out outfit after outfit as I decided on the best clothes to wear for our visit to the museum.

"It was obvious that you needed to rest. Your head needs to be clear. Linda agreed we should allow you to sleep for at least four hours," Sinn said, and I attempted to hide my anger.

"Timing is important. You shouldn't have let me sleep so

long. We have a lot to do. We need to go to the museum during the day or do you want to break into the place? That worked out so well at the school," I said, and Sinn chuckled. Linda was still absent, and I wondered where she had gone. Checking on Chloe, maybe?

"We just need to get in before they stop the visitors from entering. Linda should be able to whip up a magical spell that will make us invisible to humans. We can search for clues at the museum without prying eyes. Let's hope we find everything we need quickly. Linda said the museum is huge," Sinn said, and I nodded, taking a bite from the toast on the plate. I was famished. I took a sip from the glass of milk and fixed my eyes on Sinn.

"Where is Linda?"

"Oh, Linda…" he replied and stood, pacing in the bedroom. He smiled, but his nervousness showed.

"What's going on?"

"Nothing. She is fine. She's here, if that's what you are asking. I think she went to change Chloe's outfit and wash her up." He had barely finished talking when the door opened and Linda walked into the room.

"Finally, she wakes!" She announced dramatically, and we chuckled.

"I still think you guys should have woken me earlier. We need to get going. It takes an hour and a half to get to the museum. Even with magic, we can't pause time. It will be 4 O'clock soon," I said.

Sinn glanced at Linda, then back to me. "When does the Museum of Ancient Arts stop taking visitors?"

"6 pm. By that time, no one is allowed into the museum and everyone inside is given thirty minutes to leave," Linda replied, and he nodded silently. Then he glanced at the time.

"If we can head out at 4 pm. We should get there by 5:30,

and that should give us enough time to either find what we need or hide inside and wait for everyone to leave. Then we will search for clues without triggering any alarms," Sinn said. I had to admit it was a great idea and made me feel better about sleeping so long. Then, I realized that they were looking at me and I wondered what I had done.

"What did I do wrong this time?" I said in a voice that made me sound guilty, though I had no idea why.

"Nothing, you're still in bed, eating and delaying Sinn. He is ready to head out to the Museum of Ancient Arts. So, get your ass out of bed and get ready. You need to hit the road and I don't want to have to drag you to the car," Linda said, and we all laughed, but I knew she wasn't joking. She teased me to let me know she wasn't mad that she couldn't come and I couldn't express what her faith in me meant.

I rushed my meal, downing the milk and toast as quickly as possible because I knew I needed the strength. I had no idea how long we would be gone and I wondered if there was another test we were going to face at the museum.

It took five minutes to wash my face and change into a new outfit. I had never gotten ready so quickly in my life. Marcellus would have been proud. I was always making him wait. As I dressed up, I looked at my watch and saw it was almost 4 pm. Then, I rushed out of my bedroom and down the carpeted steps to the living room, where Sinn was waiting. He had changed into another outfit with a white dress shirt and black pants. This was another outfit that was not in Marcellus' things and I wondered if Sinn went shopping without me. I made a mental note to ask him about it later, and a quick smile graced my face as I got closer to him. I noticed that he was carrying a backpack, and it made me chuckle.

"What's funny?" He asked, with questioning eyes.

"What's with the backpack?" I asked, and Sinn glanced at it.

"Well, I've been doing a bit of research. This is like an adventure, and we need to be ready for whatever lies ahead. So, I googled essential things a person would need for a day out." As he talked, I cut him off by raising my hand.

"You googled?" I said, shocked, and Sinn nodded quickly.

"Yes, I did. Well, I admit it took a bit of getting used to. Back to what I was saying before you cut me off… using the information learned online, I found a backpack in the laundry room. I packed it with bottles of water, some candy bars, two flashlights, some chocolate bars, and a bag of chips."

"Wait, where did you get all these items? Because I know they weren't in the fridge and why are we packing like it's a picnic?" I asked, secretly admiring Sinn's quick thinking.

Linda stepped into the room. "I made a quick run to the local store and purchased them. But Sinn made the list. All I did was find them and pay for them. Now, can you guys get going?" If I knew one thing about her, it was that the last line wasn't a question. It was rhetorical, and we needed to leave before she dragged us out by our ears.

"Fine… fine. We are leaving already," I said and walked to the door, with Sinn closely behind me. We got outside, and I inhaled sharply, allowing fresh air into my nostrils. It seemed like forever since I went outside and enjoyed the smell of lavender and pine. I had several flowers in bloom and was sad I didn't have time to tend them. My garden had been one of my saving graces after Marcellus' death, and I had neglected it since my magic went on the fritz.

Sinn slipped his hands into mine and continued the walk to the car. He wasn't aware that his actions made me inhale sharply, or that it sent a shiver down my spine. His fingers warmed mine until he reached for the car door. He waited for me to get on the driver's side.

"I was waiting for you to shock me by saying you could drive already," I teased as Sinn entered the passenger side of the car and he laughed.

"Not yet, but I'm confident it is a skill I can learn easily," he shot back, and I looked at him, laughing aloud as I turned the key, starting the engine.

A minute later, we were on our way, chattering about nonsense and avoiding the obvious fear that this was another trap. That we were playing out the grand plan of the Dark God. He was the puppeteer and us, his puppets.

"You don't have to pretend. I know what you are thinking," Sinn said as I pointed to an old house I had admired growing up.

"What?"

"I know what's on your mind. Since the fiasco with the poison, you can't seem to forget that every action we take might be a trap set by the Dark God. Just remember, trap or not, this must be done."

"Fair enough, and I agree, but you are wrong. That's not what's on my mind," I replied, making a quick turn onto the highway.

"Then what is it?" Sinn asked.

"I've noticed that your outfit has changed and those are not Marcellus' clothes. Did you go shopping?"

"Without your knowledge? Is that possible?" He looked out of the window for a moment, and I shrugged.

"You were able to find your way through a Google search. Surely, you would have no problems finding your way to a clothing store."

"True. But I have always believed that women understand a man's taste and what looks good on him. I didn't get them myself. I have no money even if I wanted to. Linda got them for me. I wonder why she never told you. She said she had them at home and they were of no use. She thought they would look good on me," Sinn said, and I sighed. I wondered why Linda never mentioned it before and then decided it didn't matter. She was a good friend and was looking out for Sinn. It was just an oversight, right?

"She didn't tell you?" Sinn asked, and I glanced at him for a second before fixing my eyes on the road.

"Sure, she did. I just forgot until you mentioned it," I lied, and I didn't know why. Perhaps I didn't want more questions and thoughts as to why Linda didn't tell me and decided they were likely a gift for Marcellus that she never got a chance to give.

"Are you sure we can get to the museum before 6 pm?" Sinn asked, and I chuckled. He hadn't seen me at my best. Linda was sure I was a racecar driver in another life. Judging by the number of times I was stopped by the cops; she was likely correct.

"If I wanted to break every traffic law available on the way there, we would be getting there in a half hour. Don't worry, nobody is breaking any laws, and be rest assured that we will get there before the museum closes. We have to get there," I said, hitting the pedal. Failing wasn't an option.

CHAPTER 3

The Museum of Ancient Arts was an artistic masterpiece, every architect's fantasy. It had the flags of many of the nations in front and, in all my visits to the museum, I still couldn't name them all. I parked my vehicle in the closest stall and got out of the car, with Sinn close behind me. I looked at my wristwatch and it was 5:36 pm.

Quickly, I turned to Sinn. "I told you we would be there before the museum stops letting visitors in. We still have twenty-four minutes to get inside," I announced, and Sinn winked back.

"We have 23 minutes and counting to get inside," he said in a teasing manner, and I rolled my eyes dramatically.

"Let's go," I said, and led the way to the entrance. The railings were metal and corralled the line in a zig-zag pattern as you approached the door. It had been some time since they had a new addition to the museum. At least one that brought a sea of visitors. I looked back at Sinn and smirked at the way the backpack hung on his back.

"Why are you staring at me?" he asked.

"I can't help it. You're a demon carrying a backpack. It's kinda funny and makes you look younger. I guess I don't associate you with something so mundane," I said, and Sinn laughed.

"Then I guess I didn't do too bad, then?"

"Nope. It looks good. Plus, we may need the supplies you packed, so it was a good call," I admitted as we got closer to the door. "Bring out any metal you have on you," I said, and Sinn stopped and looked at me, confused.

"Metal? Why?" he asked.

"We have to go through a metal detector… you know… for security reasons, and having anything that's metallic on you will lead to questioning. Until you are cleared by the detector, keep everything with metal on it in the bin they provide. Do you understand?"

"Sure. But I don't have any metal on me. I don't even have a wristwatch," he announced, and I realized that he was right. He hadn't acquired anything that required a key nor did he need a knife to protect himself. Quickly, I made a mental note to get him a wristwatch when everything was over, provided that we were still alive.

We got to the main doors and walked inside. As usual, in all my visits to the museum, we had to go through the guards and a metal detector. I felt like I was in customs at the border, reminding me of my last vacation with Marcellus.

"Give the officer on the right your backpack," I said to Sinn, pointing to a female officer who indicated for Sinn to put his pack on the table. I held out my car keys as I neared the detector. This was a new experience for Sinn, and a part of me wished we came here for leisure rather than to find a cure for Chloe. We walked through the detector and Sinn watched silently as our bag was searched.

"Are you campers?" The officer asked, and I nodded,

taking a quick look at her name tag while pondering a suitable reply.

"We do go camping often. Is there a reason why you are asking, Officer McCartney?" I asked.

"Well, you have flashlights and what looks like camping supplies. I'm just asking," she said, recovering quickly after I called her name. I always wondered why people seemed so shocked when you used their name, when they wore a nametag.

"The flashlights are new. We thought we might need them if we decide to visit some secret chambers in the museum," I joked.

"You are a funny one. Well, it is a good thing we don't have any hidden chambers here, isn't it?" Officer McCartney replied, and I forced a laugh, slipping my hand into Sinn's as I glanced at the time.

"We don't have a lot of time before the museum closes. It's been nice talking to you, officer McCartney," I replied and smiled at her, turning to continue the walk into the museum before the officer could ask any more questions.

"Excuse me," Officer McCartney called, and I cursed under my breath as I turned to face her. Quickly, I hid my anger under a smile, and she smiled back. "You left your backpack," she added, raising it up, and I sighed. If she wasn't curious of our activities before, we just singled ourselves out and it was my fault for not being patient.

"Thank you so much. It was a long drive and I'm so focused on seeing the ancient art available in the museum and I'm running out of time," I said, and Officer McCartney nodded slightly. I prayed I hadn't spooked her and that she wouldn't be looking for us to leave.

"Your boyfriend doesn't talk much?" she said, looking at Sinn and he stared back at her coolly.

"I talk, officer. I just don't speak unless I am spoken to," he replied, and her eyes narrowed at his attitude.

"Fair enough," she remarked as a group of students approached the museum. "Well, work calls. But if you want to check out the ancient arts in this museum, you should check the Greek art collection and the African art collection. Those are the oldest you will find here," she said, and I nodded, pulling Sinn toward the exhibits.

"Thank you, officer. Do have a nice day," I said, but she didn't answer as the students crowded around her and her partner, overwhelming them.

"That was a close one," Sinn said, and I chuckled, still holding his hand as we walked to the heart of the museum. The words of the officer that Sinn was my boyfriend made me giggle and Sinn looked at me. Then our eyes fell on our interlocked hands and we released them. "So, what's the next step?" he asked, and I shook my head. The riddle brought us here, but there was nothing saying where we should check first.

The museum was in a circular shape. We stood in the middle and had a dozen sections we could enter and explore. Arrows marked the walls, directing the patrons to the section of their choice. Since the officer seemed to know a lot about the artifacts contained within, I decided we should take her advice.

"I think we should just visit the Greek art collection. Since we are talking about the underworld, it seems like a wise choice to start there," I said, and Sinn nodded. We followed the arrows on the walls, taking a left turn, then a right until we got to a hallway with 'Greek Art Collection' boldly written at the entrance.

"This is it," I said and entered the hall, glancing at Sinn, who looked fascinated by everything he saw. His eyes darted from a tall statue to a large tapestry.

"It is breathtaking, isn't it?" I asked, and he nodded with a smile, walking further down the hall. On the left side, there were sculptures of various Greek gods and for a second, I wondered if the craftsmen saw Zeus or Poseidon before carving them into sculptures. I moved towards the statue of Poseidon holding a trident.

"Did you know the trident is said to be one of the most powerful weapons ever forged? It was forged by the finest cyclopes too," I said with joy and turned to see Sinn watching me sternly. "What?"

"We aren't here for art lessons. Besides, do you think I don't know about the God of the seas and his powerful trident? Or do you think I have no idea about Zeus's lightning bolt? We have to look for any other clues left by Lord Ravin and we need to do that fast," he said, and his harsh words startled me. His ire was barely leashed, and I wondered why the statues of the gods seemed to bother him.

"Yes, we need to look for clues, and I hope the one Lord Ravin left is obvious." Before we could make it to the end of the exhibit, a loud alarm broke through the silence and I cursed under my breath.

"What is that?" Sinn asked.

"It's 6 PM Sinn. It's time for everyone to get out of the museum."

"But, we aren't done. Can't we ask for more time?" he asked.

"It doesn't work that way, Sinn…" I paused as his name escaped my lips and Sinn wondered what was wrong. He followed my gaze as it was fixed on a big painting on the wall. Quickly, I walked toward the painting as he followed me.

"I can't believe this," I said as we got closer, and Sinn's eyes widened in surprise when he saw what caught my eye. It was a painting of a man with dark veins around his head and another man, dressed as a peasant, standing by his side with a little bottle in his hand. There was blood all around them, like a river. A sea of people knelt before him with their hands outstretched, like they were crying for help. On the top left corner of the painting, there was a dark shadow in a cage and the mere sight of the painting sent a shiver up my spine.

"This is everything we have been looking for. There is another clue here somewhere. I can feel it," I said, and looked at Sinn who was frowning.

"But we don't have time. We have to come back another day," he said, and I shook my head. We didn't have the luxury of time and couldn't return another day. This must be done today, and I thought about how we would accomplish our goal.

"The guards will be here soon. We need to hide long enough for everyone to leave," I said casually, and Sinn faced me with a blank stare.

"How do you plan to do that without getting caught?" he asked. My mind raced over the possibilities.

"I saw a toilet in the corridor, a few meters before the entrance to this collection. We could hide in the ceiling for a few hours. Just until it gets dark and everyone is gone. We can wait for the right time to get out and look around. We will leave before we are arrested."

Sinn shook his head and reached for his pocket, bringing out a little bottle with some white liquid in it. He shook it and it turned green. "Linda said it would be green if the spell worked."

"Is this what I think it is?" I asked, knowing we had less than five minutes before some guards would come to check if there were still visitors in this area.

"It's a potion to give us invisibility for an hour. If we don't get what we want and get out in an hour, we are screwed. Linda's words, not mine," he said. I smiled and opened the potion, downing half its content before passing it to Sinn who took the rest.

"How the hell did you know we would need this?" I asked, and Sinn shrugged.

"You should be thanking Linda, not me," he said, and I began to wonder how close they were.

"Sure, I will," I said, just as two guards entered the hall. They looked around and we fell silent, watching them. They peeked behind the sculptures before meeting in the hall in front of us.

"I thought I heard voices, but there is no one here," the first guard said, and the second shrugged. This was the confirmation we needed that the spell worked, and I winked at Sinn, keeping quiet as the guards inspected a few more artifacts.

"Let's get out of here. There is no one here. If I wasn't with you all day, I would say you got drunk before coming in for your shift," the second guard said and they walked away, leaving the Greek exhibit.

"That was pretty close," I said and giggled, more out of fear than levity.

Quickly, I rushed back to the painting, running my finger over the section with the cage. Like the scrolls, it meant that the painter must have seen the stories himself or read the scrolls, but it also meant that there was a chance of a hidden message somewhere in the painting.

I moved closer to the painting again, examining it and confirming it depicted what was happening to Chloe. A perfect representation of the scrolls. "This is it," I said again, this time, fascinated by how it accurately told the story of my present predicament. But was there another clue here? I laid my hand on the side of the painting, running it over the edges for anything that felt odd. Sinn saw what I was doing, and he picked the other side, doing the same thing.

"Where is it?" I said, my voice cracked with my frustration. If there was nothing here, we had hit a dead end, and they were no closer to stopping the Dark God.

"Relax, it must be here somewhere," Sinn said, and we examined the painting again, this time, more thoroughly. With nothing at the side or front of the painting, I looked behind it, being careful not to move the painting and trigger any alarm that would send every guard in the museum our way. I ran my hand softly at the wooden edges holding the painting together and stopped when my hands caught something.

"Flashlight," I whispered, and Sinn grabbed the light from the backpack he had stashed in the corner. The invisibility potion was for us and not our gear and this meant that any guard in the corridor or anyone who entered the hall was going to see the backpack and the light. I switched it on and flashed at the back of the painting, and a smile formed on my face when I saw the old writing.

"What's that?" Sinn asked, and I pointed at it.

"It's Greek writing," I said and leaned in close.

"What does it say?" he asked again, and I read it out slowly.

"Aftós pou anazitá apantíseis prépei na gínei éna me aftón ton pínaka chrisimopoióntas ton thánato."

"What does it mean?" Sinn asked.

"He who seeks answers must become one with this painting using death."

"Does this mean one of us needs to die?" Sinn said,

slightly raising his voice and for once, I had no answer. If one of us had to die, it wasn't worth it.

"I can't answer that. But, most times, it isn't the literal meaning we should look at. This is a riddle. They don't expect everyone who solves the riddle to die while solving it."

Sinn looked at me and for a moment, we kept eye contact. The riddle played over and over in my head, and I wondered what the answer could be.

"If one of us needs to die, it should be me, not you. You still need to get the cure to Chloe," Sinn announced, and I sighed.

"Thanks for offering yourself up as a sacrificial lamb. But, nobody is dying today. Also, you need to stop talking and let me concentrate," I said as Sinn fell silent. I looked at my wristwatch. We had twenty minutes before we would be visible and a guard making rounds would see us.

"For goodness' sake!" I scowled in frustration and stood up, pacing in the hall. Then, my eyes caught another artifact, placed on a metal handle and I rushed to it, reading the name carved into the wood where it was placed.

"Whenever you are this interested in something, it is usually good news. Please tell me you have found something useful, Bree," he asked.

"I don't think the word death as used in the riddle meant we need to die to be one with painting. I think it means that we need to use something synonymous with death."

Sinn looked at me, frowning. "Imagine I am a human child. Now, explain this again," he said, and I giggled.

"I don't think a child would be interested in something as dangerous as this. But, let me explain," I paused, then continued. "The riddle says he who seeks answers must become one with the painting using death. But, I don't think it meant to actually die. It is a different kind of death. Look at this," I said, pointing to the words carved into the wood before me.

"Okay? How's that relevant to us?"

"This is a Stygius. The blade of the underworld. It is also referred to as the Stygian Blade. It is very effective in killing off any demons from the underworld, or so I heard. I think the riddle is talking about the blade. As a kid, I heard stories of witches using their blood as color for a magical painting, and I think we need to make our blood one with the painting using the Stygian blade."

"Are you sure?"

"Do you have another explanation?" I asked, and his gaze narrowed on me.

"Let's do this," he said and tried reaching for the blade, but I stopped him by putting my hand on his arm.

"Touching that blade would trigger every alarm in this place. We need to be careful. Also, we can't replace it because I don't have the magic for that. So, we need to do this quickly. As soon as we get the blade, I will cut myself and splash the blood on the painting. You will need to do the same. If it doesn't work, we are screwed."

My heart thumped in my chest. This had become a far more serious matter than ever and Sinn watched in silence as I moved closer to the Stygius. The blade of the underworld beckoned, and I was about to find out the hard way if I was wrong. As soon as I picked it up, loud alarms screeched throughout the museum. We had less than a minute before guards would swarm the hall.

"Let's do this quickly," I said and took the blade, making a quick cut on my thumb, and pressed the blood drop onto the painting. Sinn did the same, and nothing happened.

"It's not working. Are you sure there isn't a spell we need

to chant?" he asked, and I shook my head. Footsteps and distant voices echoed from every angle, and my heart raced.

"If there was a spell, I wouldn't have been able to activate it. My magic is in the off position, remember? But there isn't one. This is it," I said, and my fear escalated with the nearing voices. As the footsteps grew louder, I fixed my eyes on the painting and sucked in a breath when I noticed the blood was gone.

"Look, Sinn," I said and pointed to the painting. "Our blood, it's gone. We did this right. Why isn't it working?" I asked, and he looked as surprised as I was.

"What should we try next? We are out of time," he said as our potion wore off.

"I don't know. This was all the riddle said," I said and as I touched the painting, a bright light exploded around us and I had the sense of falling before the darkness surrounded me.

CHAPTER 4

The Darkness swirled around me. It had happened so fast my stomach rolled from the whirling. I had no idea that becoming one with the painting would involve getting sucked into it and for a second, I felt like I was Alice in Wonderland. I looked around, but I couldn't see anything. Did getting sucked into the painting induce blindness? I thought as I tried to figure out where I was. The smell was like rotting meat, like I was in a manger, but there were no sounds of any animals.

I remembered that Sinn was sucked in too and wondered where he was. "Sinn, where the hell are you?" I asked, trying not to raise my voice, but it cracked with my nervousness. The fact that I couldn't see increased my fear. "Sinn," I whispered, using my hands to make sure there was nothing around me. If he was here, we could easily use the flashlight and find our way, but his silence grated on my nerves.

Then, I heard a thumping sound, and I paused. It sounded like footsteps of someone coming closer to me and my heart beat faster. Who could it be? I wondered as my mind conjured up various beasts' intent on my destruction. I realized how safe I felt with Sinn around. *Where the hell is he? Did he get stuck in between worlds or is he in a different location? Is this some kind of test?* These questions flooded my mind as the footsteps echoed around me. Whether an enemy or a friend was yet to be determined. Uncertainty ramped up my fear. I had to use my ears to predict the direction this stranger was coming from and it made it a lot harder to hide and I wished I could see where I was going. Hell, if I knew where I was, it would help.

As I was trying to find anything in the darkness that would alert me to my location, a door opened suddenly and a flashlight blinded me. I shut my eyes, but I was relieved when I heard Sinn's voice. "Thank Goodness. I've been looking for you," he said, holding me, and I hugged him tightly. It felt like I had lost him and I didn't want to think about the fears that had plagued me minutes before.

"Take this," he said, passing me a flashlight. I moved it around the room. For the first time, I had a good look at the barn and wondered why the painting sent me to a sheep pen.

"How did I get here, and why were you somewhere else?" I asked.

"I think you would need to ask the painting. I woke up outside, on the grass."

"Where are we?" I asked, looking around, and Sinn sighed.

"You need to see for yourself," he replied, and I held his hand as he led me outside.

We exited the barn, and I looked around. It was obvious that we had gone back in time with the wooden doors and houses all around us. I turned slowly, and we were in a town fully fortified with high concrete walls and I wondered what year the painting had brought us to.

"Any ideas?" Sinn asked. The more I looked around, the more confused I was.

"Why isn't there anybody here? What the hell are we doing here?" I asked, getting frustrated as Sinn gave my hand a gentle squeeze.

"I can't answer that question, but I know that we are here for a reason and we must find out why," he said. There was a reason why we were brought here, and I prayed there was nothing dangerous lying in-wait for us.

The full moon illuminated the surrounding town, which could be a blessing or a curse. "What should we be looking for?" I asked.

"Let's look around and see what we find," he advised, and I nodded since it was the only option. A shiver ran down my spine when I realized we had no idea how we were going to get back to our world. As much as I hated to admit it, we were at the mercy of whatever inhabited the realm the painting brought us to.

"Should we hold anything white? Show that we are friendlies? Just in case?" I asked, and Sinn laughed.

"Do you think a white item of clothing would make any of the Dark God's minions think we are friendlies? Let's look around and hope we find someone willing to help us," he said, and I nodded. I needed a cure for Chloe and nothing would hinder that goal but, I was scared and had no idea what the future held for us.

I walked slowly, holding Sinn's hand. I didn't care if I was squeezing too hard or if he noticed. There was only one thought on my mind. We needed to get information and get out. And fast.

"Hello," I called out, and Sinn placed his strong arms around me and covered my mouth with his hand.

"Please, do not do that," he said sternly, and the spittle in my mouth became harder to swallow.

"Why?" I asked, curiously. But I didn't hide the fact that this whole experience was making me nervous. Note to self. Magical paintings suck.

"We don't know what is out there," he responded, as my fear escalated.

"What could be out there?" I asked as my legs became heavy. I lost the will to question him. There was definitely something dangerous out there, and I didn't want to be the one to find it. Why weren't we hiding again?

"We should hide until morning. Then we can see where we are going. Let's wait this out," I said, and Sinn didn't answer. I turned to face him and saw that he wasn't focused on me or what I was saying, but was looking ahead.

"What's that?" I asked, looking ahead and flashing my light in the direction, but there was nothing. "What did you see?" I asked again, and Sinn flashed his light in the same direction.

"Maybe it's nothing. I thought I saw a shadow," he said casually and tried to continue moving, but I froze.

"How can you act all cool when you think we might not be the only ones here and there may be a monster lurking in the shadows?" I asked.

"I'm a demon, Bree. If there was another demon close by, I would have sensed it and told you to run or hide," he said with a frown.

His words didn't reassure me that we were safe, but as I tried to talk, my eyes caught some movement. I flashed my light quickly in the direction, only to see an old man watching us sternly.

"Hello?" I called, waving a hand as the man turned and walked into a growing fog bank ahead of us.

"I'm not walking into that. He didn't say anything and this could be a trap," I said, but Sinn was already walking towards the fog. "What the hell is wrong with you?" I asked, and he continued while, angling his body to face me. It was too dangerous to be alone, so I followed him, cursing softly under my breath.

"Why are we following him without knowing who or what he is?" I asked as we entered the fog and Sinn chuckled, surprising me.

"What's funny?"

"He's a friendly, Bree," he said as we inched forward, able to see just a few meters ahead of us.

"And how did you know this?" I asked.

"I don't know… I just feel it," he replied.

"Now, you are acting weird. How did you know this is the right path?" I inquired and Sinn gave me a weak smile.

"You are forgetting that I'm also a demon," he said and held my hand tightly, navigating the fog until we got to a little house no bigger than the barn, but with the door opened.

"He's in there. He is waiting for us," he said, and I shook my head.

"There is no way I'm going in there with you," I said, and Sinn laughed. He led the way, pulling me behind him. I was too scared to stay alone, and I had no magic to protect myself. Sinn left me with no choice. As we entered the hut, I was stunned by the artistic writing on the walls. Swirling script adorned most of the surface between the packed shelves.

There were numerous roots in jars, preserved for the time they would be useful. The bottles full of various liquids reminded me of Hansen's store. With an eclectic array of everything a witch could need. The old man beckoned them inside. Was he a wizard or a witch? Either way, magic was definitely involved.

"You have wasted too much time. What took you so long to get here?" The man asked, and I glanced at Sinn, who seemed as confused as I was.

"Were you expecting us?" I asked, and he chuckled.

"Expecting you? I've been watching you since you got here. But time is not on our side. It will be here soon," he said, and I could see the fear in his eyes. Whatever he was talking about was unpleasant and I didn't need a fortune teller to know that I wouldn't want to be there when it arrived.

"Then you must know why we are here?" I asked, and the old man smiled.

"You are here for the cure, just like others who have tried and failed," he said.

"Others?"

"Yes, many others. Surely, you did not think you were the first ones who wanted to defeat the Dark God and save humanity and I doubt you will be the last. All have tried and failed, and now you must walk the same path."

"Who are you?" I asked, trying to figure out why he seemed familiar.

"Lord Ravin," he said casually, and my eyes widened. He was the reason we were here and I couldn't help but wonder how a man that looked so humble could be the great Lord Ravin.

"You seemed disappointed. You weren't expecting to meet me?" he asked, and I shrugged.

"Let's just say I was expecting something else," I said.

He got up and took a little vial with a dark brown liquid that reminded me of expresso. He handed it to me and I took it, examining its content.

"That is the reason why you are here. But, you must go now," he said.

"Wait… hold on one minute. You mean there is no test?

You are just going to hand this over to us?" I asked, incredulously.

"Getting here was the test. You became one with the painting. Do not forget to follow the moon until you find the painting that will be the gateway to your world. The Stygian blade in your bag will come in handy," he said, and I was confused. The instructions were so simple. Where was the death-defying feat or foreign puzzle? I glanced at Sinn, who opened the backpack he carried and was amazed to see the Stygian blade in it.

"I could swear that it wasn't there when we got here and I was searching for you," he said, running his fingers over the handle.

"Everything is as it should be. In my limited knowledge about your world, there are a lot of things that aren't logical but continue to happen," Lord Ravin said.

"Lord Ravin, we thank you," I said, turning to face him, but he was gone. We were all alone.

"Did you see him leave?" I asked, and Sinn shook his head.

"Lord Ravin," I said again, and there was no answer. He was a spirit and had returned to wherever he was summoned from.

"That was creepy," Sinn said.

"We need to get out of here," I said, and Sinn opened the door leading outside.

"I was hoping you would say that," he said, and we stepped out into the deserted town again. This time, the fog was gone, and the moon was at its brightest.

"I don't like this," I said, glancing around the empty town.

"Relax, I know this place is eerie quiet and we need to get the vial to Chloe, but we need to follow the moon. We shouldn't make noise until we get to the painting, become one with it, and exit this world. I want to follow his instructions."

"I agree. Let's find the painting." We had barely gone ten steps when Sinn stopped me and sniffed the air. He continued for a few seconds and I looked on, surveying my surroundings.

"What?" I asked, becoming more anxious.

"Remember when I said I would know if there was danger looming?" he said.

"Yeah?" I said, wondering why he was bringing that up now.

"Well, this is one of those moments. There is something coming our way, and it's closing in fast. Run," he said, holding my hand and pulling me as quickly as he could down the street. We sprinted down the road for a minute when a gruesome creature dropped from the sky. I realized why Lord Ravin said it would soon be here.

It was a demon that gave other demons nightmares, and Sinn paused, looking at it. There was this knowing look in his eyes, but that was a discussion for another day. The creature's red eyes focused on us as its feathered wings flapped and its large head, similar to a lion's, dripped venom from its fangs.

"Bree, don't look back. Just run. As fast as your legs will take you," he said and turned, holding my hand as we charged down the street toward a dark building.

"What's that?" I asked as he pulled me behind a shed. Our breath came in short gasps as we tried to calm ourselves and look for the creature. It appeared to have taken to the skies again, but we couldn't hear or see it.

"That's a Sphinx."

"You mean the Sphinx? The myth?" I asked, bewildered.

"On earth, you can call it a myth. But where I come from, it is as common as any other demon." This revelation made my heart stutter. How many other horrific creatures were real and wandering the underworld? The sphinx dropped down onto the road, moving its large head from side to side, searching for us. I tried to get a better look at the creature and had noticed the lion, but not the face of a woman. It was just like the stories of old, and I wondered why it had the face of a woman when she wasn't caring and would tear any human or demon to pieces.

"We can't stay here. We need to keep moving and put some distance between us and the Sphinx. It is the only way we can survive her."

This time, I planned to listen to Sinn. He had more understanding of the creature than I did, and I wondered if we could outrun it. How fast did she fly?

"Now," he said, and I sprinted as fast as my legs could carry me.

"Follow the moon," I whispered, glancing up as I ran. There was a moment when I believed we would make it out of the deserted town. Then a force hit me from behind, sending me onto my stomach and some yards off the road.

"Bree, are you okay?" Sinn asked, helping me to my feet.

I didn't see what hit me, but my arm felt numb, and Sinn placed his hands on my shoulder as we tried to run again. But, this time, it was too late. Before we could move, the sphinx landed some yards ahead of us, her eyes fixed on us like a predator looking for its next meal.

"There is nowhere else to run. You will be mine," she said in a calm voice, but the ground shook as she spoke. Sinn used his body to shield me, but I stepped out, attempting to stand beside him. But Sinn grabbed me.

"Get behind me. I can't protect you if she decides to attack head on. A sphinx shows no mercy to anyone."

"That's why you have to let me lead. We attack her

together. That's the only way to outmaneuver her," I argued and Sinn pursed his lips. He knew I wouldn't back down when my mind was made up. "Is there any special way to kill it?" I asked, and Sinn shook his head.

"I don't think there is a way to kill the sphinx. From what I've heard, you need to outsmart her. Make her feel you are wiser than her. That could make her angry and cause her to feed on herself."

My eyes widened. "She will feed on herself? How do we do that?"

Sinn shrugged. "I avoid the sphinx."

"I have an idea," I said, as he frowned. I didn't blame him for thinking the worst, and my idea wasn't going to endear him to me.

"You need to fight the Sphinx. Just don't die," I said casually, and Sinn scoffed.

"That's your plan?" he asked, and I shook my head.

"I just need you to fight with the creature and leave the rest to me," I said with confidence, and Sinn sighed. "Trust me," I said and faked a smile. Before I could explain any further, the creature charged at us. Sinn dropped the backpack and rushed toward the sphinx and I hoped he was a good fighter. That demon could rend him limb by limb if he wasn't careful.

I picked up the backpack and opened it, looking inside. A smile formed on my face when I saw the Stygius; the blade of the underworld in the bag, and I hoped this weapon was as powerful as legends boasted it to be. I glanced at Sinn as he interacted with the creature and he was doing quite well, dodging its attacks. I admired that he was using his light weight and speed to his advantage.

"For a legendary creature with hundreds of stories, you are pretty slow," I said loud enough for the sphinx to hear and she scowled in frustration. Her face reddened in anger, causing her to charge at Sinn. He waited till the last second, and when she was close, he rolled away, avoiding her attack. I chuckled as the sphinx ran head-on into a carriage that sat by the roadside.

"You are too clumsy, and this is getting boring. Jeez, do you at least have some popcorn if I am forced to watch this pathetic excuse for a show?" I shouted again. The monster howled in anger and renewed the vigor of her attack on Sinn.

"What are you doing?" Sinn asked and I pointed at the creature, charging at him once again. All I needed from him was concentration. If he was injured too soon, it would spell the end for both of us, and I needed the fight to last long enough for the plan to work.

"Just focus," I told him as he avoided another blow that could have torn him apart. The sphinx was getting frustrated that he was avoiding her attacks and I wondered if Sinn had any other moves, he could use to infuriate her further.

"I'm really going to enjoy killing you," the creature said and tried to grab Sinn with her outstretched claws, but he evaded her reach once more. He avoided her attacks with precision, and I assumed that he had some battle experience. I admired his courage and conviction in the face of this dangerous foe.

"Is this how you exact dominance? Making empty threats?" I asked, and laughed aloud. The sphinx looked at me for the first time, keeping eye contact for a while. I knew she was pissed and while that was bad for me, it was also good.

She charged at Sinn and tried to squash him into the ground with one of her legs. But she was slow, and Sinn jumped to the other side with a smile on his face. As I laughed, the sphinx turned 180 degrees and hit Sinn hard with her wings, sending him into the wall of a nearby home, which collapsed as his body slammed against it. My voice became heavy and my mind raced. The sphinx was also a creature that could think, adapt, and right now, her first attack had gotten to Sinn, and he moved from side to side, obviously in pain. There was a clean cut on his head and blood flowed from the wound on his forehead, covering the side of his face.

"You think you can be defensive and dodge my attacks forever? I must admit, I underestimated you and I thought this was going to be an easy kill and eat situation. But you surprised me, and for that, I will make your deaths more creative. You have earned that," she said and walked slowly towards Sinn who was standing again. Her wings stretched wide, making her appear angelic and evil.

If this was a tactic to look bigger before her prey, it was working on me. She walked light-footed, her sharp claws becoming visible as she neared Sinn. I looked at him as my eyes filled with tears, hoping this wouldn't be the last time we would be together. His eyes met mine as the creature closed in and then, Sinn winked at me and broke into a loud laugh.

"You think that's all I've got? You underestimate me," he said and laughed harder again. The Sphinx shrieked angrily, and she charged at him. Sinn jumped away, and she slammed into the wall, shrieking as she tried to regain her position.

Sinn rushed to my side, breathing heavily. "If you have a plan, this is where you tell me about it," he said, watching the creature, whose large weight was making it harder for her to stand up easily.

"The plan is to make her frustrated until she becomes clumsy and then use this," I said, opening the bag and exposing the Stygian blade to Sinn. "We could use the blade when she is in a rage. She doesn't see me as a threat. She wouldn't see it coming," I said, but Sinn wasn't convinced. He looked, and the sphinx was still down, giving us more time to plan. There was no way to outrun the creature. Our legs couldn't match the speed of the sphinx and fighting was our only option. That and dying, which was not an option I wanted to contemplate.

"What happens if she catches you with the blade? She hasn't lived this long by being foolish," he said, and I nodded in agreement.

"But she relies on her strength more than her wisdom, and that's what we are banking on," I said as the creature stumbled to its feet, turning to face us.

"This joke has gone on for too long," I said, and watched the creature walk slowly toward us. "If you were as powerful as the stories said you were, you would have killed us easily. But here we are, healthy and bored. I will tell everyone that the sphinx is just like every other demon. Clumsy, weak, and can't defeat a human who lacks the ability to defend herself," I added, as steam came out of her nostrils. If she wasn't angry before, she was livid now. She wanted our heads on a platter, starting with mine.

The creature charged at us. This time, she was faster. Sinn took the blade before I could say anything and ran to the other side of the road, hoping to distract the creature, but it didn't work. She didn't take the bait to run after Sinn. Her eyes remained on me as she charged, and my heart skipped a beat.

I ran as fast as my legs would carry me, knowing I didn't have the battle training Sinn had. I wouldn't be able to dodge her attack. She was going to break me in two like a twig. I ran, not bothering to look back as it would only slow me down. Besides, I was scared enough. *Why hasn't she caught up with me?* I thought, knowing she was fast enough to have my head detached from my body by now. Then I did the one thing I hated to do when running from something that scared the hell out of me, I turned.

My heart froze when I saw the sphinx with the backpack. A knowing smile formed on her face. This was her plan all along. Sinn got to my side as tears fell from my eyes. We both looked at the Sphinx and everything we came for was in her hands.

"This doesn't leave this realm, not now or ever," she said, bringing out the little vial given to us by Lord Ravin. The only cure to the Dark God's curse on Chloe.

"Noooo," I said and charged after her, but Sinn pulled me, stopping me from charging at the creature who had just made another journey useless. I watched on as she placed the vial on the ground and smashed it to pieces. The only cure for Chloe dried up into the soil and I cried, hard.

"This is the same thing you wanted her to do. Act on your anger and become clumsy. You need to get a grip on yourself, Bree," Sinn said, and I shook my head. All I wanted in that moment was the Sphinx's head on a pole. I saw red. She had to die for taking the only cure that could save my daughter. I lost hope and my anger escalated. I charged at her, escaping Sinn's grip and she smirked, watching me as I got closer to her and within range for a lethal blow. I had nothing, no weapons or spells to save or defend me. I closed in and the sphinx raised her hand, bringing her claws hard in my direction as she tried to cut me into halves.

"How dare you? How could you do something so cruel?" I said as I jumped back, crying out in pain when I realized I didn't totally escape her strike and my blood leaked from my shoulder. It stained the jacket that surrounded the torn flesh.

"Aren't you the cry baby now?" The sphinx said and licked her claws. She savored the taste of my blood and smiled at me. "I'm going to enjoy killing you. It has been a long time since a victory has tasted as sweet as this one and I must say, you put up a fight. But sadly, you still need to die," she said, and charged toward me.

Where the hell is Sinn, anyway? I thought as I realized that he wasn't close by nor had I seen him since I escaped his grip. *Has he left me to my fate?* I pondered as the creature got closer. There was no way I would avoid any attack she planned to throw at me and, in that moment, I knew this was the end for me.

"Goodbye, human," the sphinx said, and I shut my eyes, picturing Chloe's face one last time and I chuckled. Laughing at the cruelty of fate was the only thing I could do at that time. I had no strength to cry and my shoulder was killing me.

"Noooo," the sphinx screamed, and I opened my eyes to see her frozen. I never read anything about a sphinx having a change of heart and wondered why she hadn't flattened me. She turned slowly and backed away from me to reveal the Stygius blade, buried deep in her back.

"Sinn," I said as I smiled again. I stood up, holding my shoulder as the pain was increasing by the minute. As I tried to walk, the sphinx took flight, swooping through the air, before I saw Sinn. "I thought you left me," I said and rushed to his side, smiling as he wrapped his hands around me.

"Is she gone?" I asked.

"She isn't done yet. That isn't the way to hell. She needs to go down," he said, and a big O formed on my lips. We looked up as the sphinx came crashing to the earth.

"How did you get hold of the blade?" The sphinx asked and before we replied, she transformed from a creature into a young woman, but her legs were still that of a lion with large claws.

We walked towards her and she tried to move away, but the blade was still in her back and it made her weak and powerless. Sinn moved closer to her and pinned her to the ground.

I remembered how she destroyed the only cure for Chloe, and my blood boiled in rage. "I wish we could kill her slowly," I said, not hiding my feelings, and Sinn looked at me for a moment.

"That's fair enough. But you would be wasting your time. You would just be punishing this body. The Sphinx will return when there is another attempt to get a cure. She is a demon, not a human."

"Then what do we do?" I asked, and Sinn glanced at the creature. A once powerful sphinx now looked helpless and weak. "Step back."

"What?"

Suddenly, his eyes became blood red, and he looked at me for a second before focusing on the creature before him. Dark horns grew from his head and from his back sprouted bat-like wings. They flapped several times before his hand transformed. His fingers had claws and Sinn drew a line on the Sphinx forehead as she screamed in pain. Then, he placed his thumb on her head and brought his mouth lower, almost to the Sphinx's mouth.

"Noooo," she screamed as a dark smoke left her mouth into Sinn's mouth. This went on for a couple of seconds and as soon as the smoke stopped, the sphinx disintegrated leaving the Stygian blade and Sinn stood up slowly. He turned to face me and my heartbeat took on an erratic staccato. He walked towards me as I took some steps backward.

"Sinn? Is that you?" I asked, looking around for an escape

plan just in case Sinn had gone rogue. He knelt down, and I jumped back.

"Arrrgghhhh," he shouted, and I watched in silence as the wings went back into his body and the horns disappeared. He looked at me and this time, he looked like Sinn and not the demon that he was some minutes before.

"What was that?" I asked, not moving from where I was.

"I shifted to my demon side to get more information from the Sphinx."

"Why didn't you just ask?"

"You think she would willingly share whatever she knew?" he asked.

That was true. She was dying and had no reason to give us any information, especially since we had killed her. "So, what did you find out?" I asked as Sinn got to his feet and approached me.

"I am sure this won't come as a surprise, but it's all bad news."

"Spill it. I've had a lot of things not go as planned today and this one won't hurt like losing the cure."

Sinn fixed his eyes on me. "Everyone has been affected by the same curse."

"What do you mean by everybody?" I asked immediately.

"Remember my mother?"

"Yes, the goddess of wealth, Aje," I replied, and Sinn nodded.

"The information I extracted was that she and the other gods have been cursed by the same magic. Every God has been cursed by the Dark God."

I could sense the pain in Sinn's words, but I didn't understand how the Dark God could achieve such a feat. "Are you sure that information is correct? I mean... if the Dark God can curse every God still alive, then why doesn't he just take over, become the ultimate God and rule the world with brute force, bringing chaos whenever he pleases?"

Sinn frowned. Perhaps my question didn't make sense to him or I didn't understand, but it seemed logical that the Dark God would want to rule when he had the power to curse every God.

"It isn't that simple, Bree. The Gods are cursed, but that doesn't mean they are powerless. It just means that they grow weaker by the day and the one thing keeping them strong is the prayers of their followers. The prayers of humans go a long way. This is why the Dark God wants to merge the worlds. With that, he can control this world —," as Sinn tried to explain further, I interrupted him as it clicked into place.

"And if he takes control of this world, and the underworld is merged with the human world, there would be nobody to pray to the gods anymore, and this would lead to their death."

Sinn nodded.

"This is not good," I said as I realized that the Dark God's ultimate plan that was much bigger than Chloe. The merging of the worlds was catastrophic and my daughter was just caught in the web of a Dark God's hunger for power.

"We are sitting on a time bomb and right now, everything is working for the Dark God. The other Gods are weak and they can't form a united front against him. However, his goal will not be achieved if this world doesn't merge with the underworld. As they weaken, the Gods will die. The older gods will lose power and die, until the most powerful God follows, leaving the Dark God as the supreme ruler and no force from now till eternity will be able to thwart him."

This was a disaster. We were closer to being enslaved to a Dark God and his grand plan was still in play. The pain in Sinn's voice was still evident, and I understood. I would be in pain too if I found out that my mother had been cursed by the

Dark God and would die if he achieved his goal of merging both worlds together.

"This is bigger than just Chloe, and we need to plan effectively," I said as my shoulder sent waves of pain through my body and I grimaced.

"We need to get that looked at," Sinn said, and I looked at my shoulder. The blood had dried up, and the injury was not as deep as I had feared.

"We need to get out of here," I replied, and Sinn nodded. He gave me his hand, and I took it. We walked together, taking the Stygian blade and the backpack, which had nothing but candy and chocolates left.

"Care for a candy bar?" Sinn asked, and I took one from him. We needed to focus on the positives. We weren't dead or in the stomach of a sphinx, and we had learned a bit more about the Dark God's plan. We followed the moon until we came to a stream and on a rock by the banks was the same painting as we saw in the Museum of Ancient Arts. Quickly, I made a quick cut to my thumb and splashed the blood on the painting, and Sinn did the same. I turned toward him as everything went black.

CHAPTER 5

*L*ight emerged from the darkness, and then we were once again at the Greek collection hall, by the painting. It was no longer nighttime like when we were sucked into the painting, but a sunny day with tourists all around. I paused and looked at Sinn, and he stared back at me, confused as I was. The shocked reaction from everyone around us never came, and I realized that the invisibility spell was still working.

"The invisibility spell still works. We need to move fast because we have less than a minute before we become visible," I said to Sinn, and a tourist turned toward me. It was obvious that she heard voices, but couldn't see who was talking. "Quickly," I whispered again, stretching my good arm to Sinn, and we ran out of the Museum, passing officer McCartney who was once again swarmed with tourists. We got to the car, and I rushed to the driver's side.

"Can you drive?" Sinn asked, and I paused for a moment.

"Can you?" I shot back.

"I haven't learned that yet," Sinn said.

"Then I guess I don't have a choice. I have to make the

drive home," I replied, and unlocked the car doors. I sat down with a groan as my shoulder burned, then started the engine of my Toyota Corolla as soon as Sinn put his seatbelt on.

The pain in my shoulder was like acid on my skin by the time I pulled into the driveway an hour and a half later and Linda rushed out, looking concerned.

"Thank the Gods," she said as I exited the car and she ran to my side, supporting my weight. Sinn came to my free side, and they assisted me into the house.

"What took you guys so long?" Linda asked after assisting me to a sofa in the living room, and Sinn rushed to get the first aid kit in the bathroom.

"We left yesterday, Linda. You speak as if we have been gone for weeks," I said with a smile, but she didn't return the smile.

"You weren't gone for weeks, but you guys have been gone for days," she replied, just as Sinn returned with the first aid kit.

"What?" he exclaimed. Linda's words shocked us both, and I fixed my eyes on her, wondering if she had said that right.

"We only spent one night in a painting. We got out before dawn and we are back here. Although, it was daytime when we got here. How could we have been gone for days?" I asked, but Linda shrugged.

"I can't explain why. But I can tell you that you have been gone for three days."

Sinn looked at me, as shocked as I was. I had no logical explanation for what happened.

"It's all about magic. Time must move differently in the painting. Can we fix my shoulder now?" I said, sitting up, and Linda grabbed the supplies from the first aid kit and got to work. Twenty minutes later, I was all stitched up and the look on Linda's face was expectant. There would be no rest until I told her everything that had happened.

"Where is the cure?" she asked, looking at us, and Sinn shook his head. "What happened?"

"We encountered a sphinx. She destroyed the cure as we fought with her," I said, and Linda's shoulders sagged.

"Are we talking about the same sphinx? Body of a Lion, face of a woman and wings of an eagle, type of sphinx?" she asked, sitting up.

"The very same one. While our journey to find the cure didn't go as planned and we returned empty-handed, we also got some information," I said, looking at Sinn, wondering if talking about him revealing his demon side was a wise choice.

"What is it?" Linda asked, and I kept quiet for a moment, trying to lie down. "I will conjure some spells for the pain soon," she added, and I smiled at her.

"We found out the Dark God's grand plan and to simplify, it isn't good. We can't allow him to merge both worlds. It would be the end for all of us," I said, and Linda still looked confused.

"Now, I'm lost and you need to explain," she said, and I glanced at Sinn.

"Help her understand," I said.

"Well, we found out that Chloe and I weren't the only ones cursed by the Dark God. He has cursed every single God, old and young. The only reason why they aren't dead yet is because of the humans. The prayers and worship given to these gods replenish their strength every day, and it keeps them strong enough to stall the curse. But, when the worlds merge together." Sinn trailed off and looked at me, just as Linda fixed her eyes on him.

"Oh, God!" she exclaimed, and I knew she had figured it

out. "There would be no humans to worship the gods, and there would be no way for them to replenish their energy. They would die," she said in whispers. The fact that I didn't deny her assertions broke Linda's heart, and she stared at me as tears filled her eyes. Linda was an emotional person, too emotional in fact, and I moved closer to her, wrapping my hands around her. "They would all die," she whispered again and this time, the tears came, pouring down her eyes.

"It's okay. We won't let that happen."

"How?" she asked, looking at me with tear-filled eyes.

"It's pretty obvious that we are humanity's last hope. There's no one who will believe this crazy story. We have to find a way and defeat the Dark God. Even if it's the last thing we do. Some days ago, both of you asked me a question about my choice of action, what I wanted to do and who I would choose to save between Chloe and the world. Then, I was scared for my life, and thoughts about saving the world meant that I wouldn't be there for Chloe. I wasn't looking at the big picture. Now, I know better. This is our responsibility. If we visit the underworld, I might not make it out alive. But, if my sacrifice will bring stability to this world and save my daughter and those of other parents from damnation, I will give it."

Sinn and Linda looked at me in silence, and I smiled when I noticed that her tears had dried up. "That was one hell of a speech," Linda said, and we all chuckled.

"You could fit the role of a commander, taking his soldiers to war when the odds are against them," Sinn said, and I smiled. Although, comparing myself to a commander felt too extravagant. I understood Sinn had used a comparison he could relate to and I appreciated it.

"So… commander Breena. How do we proceed?" Linda asked, standing up and faking a salute as she teased me.

Then, a crazy idea dropped into my mind. "I know that look. It usually means you will say something I will hate," Linda said, sitting up, and I chuckled. She knew me better than anyone, and she wasn't wrong.

I glanced at the clock in the living room and noticed that it was almost noon. My stomach grumbled, reminding me that the last time I ate was three days ago, before I entered the magical painting.

"Stop keeping up the suspense. Talk," Linda said again, and jerked me from my thoughts. I fixed my eyes on her.

"Well," I said, interlocking my fingers. "You guys aren't going to like what I'm about to say."

Linda frowned at me for a moment, then said, "does this plan you just cooked up get the job done? Will it lead to the imprisonment of the Dark God?" she asked, and I thought about it again, knowing that my choice of words mattered.

"I think it's our best chance so far, if that's what you are asking me. Honestly, it's the best I've got," I said.

"Then shoot. We are all ears," Sinn said, taking his seat on the closest sofa.

"We need to ask someone who knows more information about the Dark God and what happened in the past," I said.

"But who? I don't know anyone, and I doubt Sinn does."

"I realize that, Linda. But you didn't let me finish. The best person we can ask for more information is the one who gave us the most credible info in the first place."

Linda and Sinn looked at me, still confused.

"How else do you want me to say this? We need to talk to someone who knows more. The only person who knows more told us about Baldwin and his information sent us to the Museum of Ancient Arts. Do you understand where I'm going now?" I said, raising my voice slightly as my frustration piqued.

"No way. You can't possibly want to breach the world between humans and the underworld. Trust me, you don't want to do that," Sinn said, and Linda looked at him for a moment, then she turned and faced me. I knew she was connecting the dots, and the only way to move forward was to let her figure it out herself.

"Don't tell me you mean what I think you do?" she said after a while, and I felt a lump in my throat. I needed Linda's support, and she sounded scared of my idea. Rightfully so. It was nuts.

"What are you thinking about?" I asked casually.

"If I'm understanding this correctly, the person you are talking about is Lord Ravin. You want to talk to Lord Ravin," she said, frowning at me.

"Guys… that's the best option we have right now. We need to know more, and Lord Ravin has all the knowledge we need. We just need to summon him for a short while, discuss the most feasible plan available, and send him back," I said and shrugged. Sinn stood up and his growl startled me.

"You don't want to do that. You don't understand the consequences that could follow that kind of summoning. It's too dangerous. I can't be a part of that," Sinn said sternly. I looked at Linda, hoping that she would support me in summoning Lord Ravin, but her facial expression was disappointing.

"What are the consequences of summoning Lord Ravin? What could go wrong?" I asked.

"Everything! Everything could go wrong. In fact, everything will go wrong," Sinn said and charged toward me, stopping before me. I could feel his breath on my face, but the last time, it had sent shivers of anticipation. Now, it brought fear, sending a series of chills down my spine.

Sinn noticed my reaction to his outburst, and he took a

few steps backward, taking deep breaths. Then, he said, "I'm sorry I spoke to you like that. But you need to understand that there are some lines you don't cross. This is something you should fear. I'm sure you have heard stories of witches who did it, but you didn't hear of the consequences of their actions."

"You still haven't told me what the consequences of summoning Lord Ravin would be," I said calmly, and Sinn pursed his lips. It was obvious he didn't want to share those consequences. He looked me over from my head to my feet. He didn't try to hide the anger on his face.

"Linda, please make her see reason. Make her understand that this is something no witch should do," he said, facing Linda. She watched us in silence as he began to pace the living room, muttering under his breath. I turned to face Linda, not knowing what to expect from her.

"It's too dangerous, Bree. It's not something you have done before, and you don't know how to summon someone from the underworld. This isn't like summoning a demon, you know?" she said and I nodded.

"You are right. I have never summoned the dead before. But I believe there is a way to go about it in the Book of Lost Shadows. I'm sure it's there."

"Have you forgotten that dark magic is forbidden by the coven? Elder Sabrina wouldn't be able to save us if we got caught. Chloe would die without us to care for her." Linda reminded me.

"Do you think we can defeat the Dark God without the use of dark magic? Do you really believe we can do that?" I asked and suppressed my smile when Linda went silent. It was obvious that she was mulling over my last question, and this gave me time to steal a glance at Sinn. He was still frowning.

"Fine, I agree desperate times require desperate measures. But we need to hear Sinn out and find out what he is afraid of. Why doesn't he want you to do it?" Linda said, and we both turned to Sinn.

"You seriously want to go down this path?" he said, with a clear reprimand in his voice. "Since you want to know what can happen, I will list them for you." With this, he crossed his arms and paced around the living room, stopping behind the sofa that stood in front of Linda and me. His ire was clear and I knew I wouldn't like what he was about to say. I pushed the negative thoughts out of my head when he cleared his throat. "The first problem is your chance of failure. There is a very high probability that you will summon a demon, one stronger than the sphinx, one who is at the beck and call of the Dark God. This will not only place our lives in danger but also give this creature the opportunity to kill Chloe, because that's what I would do if I were the Dark God."

"Is that all?" I asked, and Sinn shook his head. He didn't like me opposing him or how I disregarded the dangers involved. If the chance of summoning the wrong demon was the only thing I had to be scared of, then I was ready to take my chances.

"Isn't that enough to be scared?" He shot back, and I smiled. That didn't sit well with him.

"Am I scared of summoning the wrong demon? Yes. I hope I don't have to fight any demons. But, in the event that I do, you are here to protect me and I know you are quite good at it," I said, and winked at him. Linda looked at me for a second, noticing the wink, and she had to be wondering what happened when we were in the painting.

"That isn't all..." Sinn trailed off, and I sighed. He should have read the signs at this point that nothing other than

Chloe's consciousness could stop me from summoning Lord Ravin, and I wondered what he had to say this time.

"What is it now?" I asked.

"Summoning Lord Ravin would merge both worlds together; the underworld and the human world. This will create a loop that he would pass through to this world and give you the opportunity to talk to him. But this loop stays open while you talk to him, and many demons could pass through. You could send an army to Drima Falls and while fighting one demon might be easy, I will be no match for hordes of them, and I might not be able to protect you."

I could see the concern in Sinn's eyes and I wished there was another way, but there wasn't. "I'm sorry, Sinn. We have to do this. We have to take the chance. So, you are either with us all the way or not. Choose," I said, knowing he was not going to leave me hanging. I hated to do this to him, considering everything he had done to help me and Chloe, but I was out of options.

Sinn looked at me for a while, and then returned to the couch, flopping into it with a loud sigh. "Seems I've got no choice. Do what you have to do."

I smiled and walked to the attic. I had a summoning spell to perform.

CHAPTER 6

y shoulder sent waves of lightning through my body and I had to rest against the wall as I got closer to the carpeted steps that led to the bedrooms. My face beaded in sweat and my fingers were going numb.

"You need to rest before we do anything. You look like you are about to pass out," Sinn said, and I shot him a deadly look. My anger at him for stating the obvious made me ignore the concern in his voice.

"I'm not resting until I have talked to Lord Ravin," I said, raising my voice a little as Sinn leaned closer to me. The sweat had my clothes clinging to my body, but I wasn't going to back down, not now. It felt like my head was splitting into two, and I knew my fever was hitting dangerous proportions.

"She is burning up," Sinn said as he touched my head and Linda rushed to my side. She touched my head as well and had a concerned look on her face.

"Let me see," she said, checking the wound on my shoulder and I groaned in pain as she inspected the cut. "There is no sign of infection. But your fever is rising and if we don't get that down soon, you will pass out."

"I'm not doing anything until I've talked to Lord Ravin," I said again and tried to walk up the steps that led to the bedroom, but my legs were too weak to hold me and I ended up grabbing the rail for support.

"Fine, I'll get the book for you," Sinn said, and this time, I didn't argue. I removed the locket hanging around my neck and placed it on his hand, watching weakly as he raced up the carpeted steps to the corridor. Then, he reached up and yanked the pull-down stairs leading to the attic. It took seconds for him to disappear and reappear with the Book of Lost Shadows in his hands.

"I've got it," he said aloud, waving it to my face. But I could no longer see him clearly.

"Breena? Breena!" I heard faintly as the darkness swallowed me.

~

"Breena, wake up. WAKE UP!"

My eyelids fluttered as I attempted to respond. I wasn't resting against the wall by the steps, I was in my bedroom, on my bed, and under the covers. I smelled like strawberries and cologne and I wondered what had happened. I looked around for a moment, but there was nothing out of the ordinary. Everything was in place, just as I had left them before going to the Museum of Ancient Arts. Then, my eyes fell on some clothes on the floor and I felt a lump in my throat. It was my outfit from my trip to the museum, which I had on until I got dizzy downstairs. I pulled back the covers, eyeing the pink pajamas. Who changed my outfit for me?

"Linda? Sinn?" I called out, expecting Linda was the one who went to the trouble of changing my outfit. The thought that it could be Sinn didn't worry me, especially since he had seen me naked, but I didn't like feeling vulnerable. "Linda! Sinn!" I called again, this time, raising the pitch of my voice until I heard some footsteps running up the stairs. Soon, they both burst into my bedroom, breathing heavily.

"What's going on? Why am I dressed in this?" I asked, looking from Sinn to Linda.

"Well, you kinda passed out. You had a fever," Sinn said quickly.

"Had?" I asked again.

"Yeah, you had a fever because the cut in your shoulder was poisonous. It was from a sphinx. It wasn't just any injury, but while you were unconscious, I removed the sphinx venom from your body. It was slowly consuming your essence from the inside out. I also changed your outfit and cleaned your body with a towel, and sprayed you with some perfume and oils I found in the drawers over there," Linda said, pointing to the set of drawers beside a big mirror I used to check my make-up before heading out for the evening. That left me with one question. How had they had enough time to do all this?

"How long have I been unconscious?" I asked, looking at Sinn as he walked to a little table beside my bed, grabbing my wristwatch.

"That would be about nineteen hours," he said, setting the watch back on the table again. I blinked praying I heard that wrong.

"Nineteen hours? How could you let that happen? I have to summon Lord Ravin!" I yelled and scrambled out of bed. "What's the time now?" I asked, looking at Sinn, and he sighed as he glanced at the wristwatch.

"6:47 am."

I remembered that the last thing I wanted to do was to talk to Lord Ravin and get something to eat. That was noon on

Thursday, the day before. How was I out for so long? I mentally kicked myself.

"We don't have the luxury of time. We need to act fast," I said and walked to the wardrobe, stopping when I remembered that Sinn was still in the room. I looked at him and then at the door. It took him a moment, but he got my message.

"Oh—ohh… I'm gonna wait outside for you guys. I will let you change," he said, and it was obvious that he was feeling uneasy. I watched him as he walked outside and closed the door behind him. Then, quickly, I opened the wardrobe doors and searched for an outfit, selecting a flowery dress shirt and capris.

"You should be thanking Sinn, you know?" Linda said, and I turned towards her. I said nothing for a moment, slipping into the dress shirt and closing the zipper at the back of the pants after I pulled them on.

"Why?"

"He spent most of the hours you were unconscious by your side, holding your hand." I paused and looked at Linda as her words sunk in.

"Really?" I asked as a smile formed on my lips and Linda nodded.

"I tried to make him leave, but he wouldn't. He was like your guardian angel. Maybe it wasn't a terrible idea summoning him after all," she said and we both laughed. Once again, my mind drifted to her earlier statement, and I giggled, ignoring the fact that Linda might be watching me. I took a deep breath, and another smile formed on my face when I could smell his scent. The sweet savory smell of his body was unique, and it filled my nostrils and calmed my nerves.

"Now, you are praising Sinn. The day I summoned him;

you almost had my head on a pike. Besides, he stayed in the room because he is bound to protect me, not because he is like a human man who wants to ensure that I was safe."

"I strongly doubt that," Linda countered as I got closer to the door, causing me to turn and face her. I scoffed and looked at her with one eyebrow raised. "Did you become a seer, too? You can see emotions now?" I asked.

"He acts like he cares about you. That's what I'm trying to tell you. It is pretty obvious he has feelings for you. But if you think he is obligated to protect you and nothing more, I won't argue with you," Linda said.

Why would he care about me? His kind cared about no one, but themselves and for a moment, I wondered if I would have waited for nineteen hours beside his bed. I could not answer that question and once again, my mind returned to my plan to summon Lord Ravin.

"Can we drop that for now and talk about something else?" I asked, trying not to let my frustration show.

"Yeah, sure."

I sighed in relief. She was just being observant, and I didn't blame her. But, if Sinn truly cared about me, time would tell. "We have to summon Lord Ravin today. Right now," I said, and crossed my arms. My voice was stern, and I hoped Linda wouldn't argue with me.

"Then, we need to go downstairs," she said, walking past me and opening my bedroom door with one swift move. I joined her in the corridor and for a moment, my legs felt weak as I looked at Chloe's door. The longer she was in that condition, under the curse of a God, the more pain I felt. "Do you want to see her?" Linda asked in whispers and I looked at her, fighting the tears that threatened my eyes. As much as it was going to hurt, I needed to see my daughter. It had been days since I saw her and though that wasn't my fault, nor would she notice, I felt guilty.

"I need to see her," I said, and walked to Chloe's bedroom before Linda could say anything. She silently walked to my side, placing a hand around my shoulder as we both walked into the bedroom. Chloe was the same as she was four days ago. Still unconscious, the veins around her body looked darker as I moved closer to her. There was no way to hold back the tears filling my eyes. The cure was in my hand, and I let it slip through my fingers. My arrogance could cost my daughter her life. I couldn't imagine the discomfort and pain she was in. The only thing that had changed since I last saw her was her outfit, and it had Linda written all over it.

"Thank you," I mouthed to her, and she wrapped her hands around me.

"We will save her, Bree. We will save her," she said calmly, and I cried. Being in the room brought back memories. I looked towards the table on the left end of the room. It still had Chloe's laptop on it, and that was where she would have been if she wasn't out working with Ravana. My eyes fell on the painting on the wall, a hobby she loved whenever she was bored. Though blurred through the water it was still beautiful.

I wiped my tears focusing on the task ahead. The analog clock in Chloe's room read 7:50 am, and it was an indication that time wasn't going to wait for me. "Let's go. We have got work to do," I said, sniffing as I looked at Chloe. I walked to the door, and Linda held my hand as we entered the hallway. There was no sign of Sinn, but I knew he was probably in the living room waiting for me or in the kitchen fixing me something to eat. At this point, my stomach grumbled at the thought of food.

"You haven't had anything decent to eat in a while,"

Linda said. I inhaled deeply at the scrumptious smell. My mouth watered, and I turned quickly to Linda, and the look in my eyes stopped her. It was soothing and comforting, but I couldn't place what it was.

"Can you smell that?" I asked, and she laughed. Her giggles surprised me.

"Of course, I can smell it. I was the one who made it."

"What is it?" I asked again, curiously.

"It's no particular scent. It was made with magic, and the best part about it is that you get to smell whatever you think is pleasant or soothing. So, it's you. If you want a mouth-watering smell, you have got it. Want a floral smell? It will happen in seconds," she said, and I thought about the strong smell of springtime. I concentrated and there was a sudden smell of spring around me and I chuckled.

"That is good," I said and walked to the carpeted steps. As I took them one at a time, the need to get the Book of Lost Shadows replayed in my mind. Soon, I waved the thoughts aside and reached the living room, walking toward the sofas where Sinn was seated. His look was speculative. I glanced at Linda and she had the 'appreciate him' look all over her face.

Quietly, I walked up to him and cleared my throat. "I know I may have come off a little hostile toward you. I didn't mean to snap at you. I'm sorry."

"You were just waking up. I know you aren't mad at me. I totally understand," he said with a smile.

"Thank you," I said.

"Sure… yeah… we are cool," he said with a nod.

"Linda told me you were my guardian angel while I was unconscious. Thank you for that, too. I appreciate you looking out for me," I said, and Sinn glanced at Linda.

"Yes, I stayed with you for a long time, but you should be thanking Linda. I had no idea what to do when you passed out and if she wasn't a witch, and a good one at that, we might have lost you," I could swear that I sensed concern in his voice. It was quite clear, but I decided not to mention it and glanced at Linda.

"You don't need to thank me. You would have done the same," she said calmly, and I nodded. She was right. We had been friends for so long, that there was nothing I wouldn't do for her.

"I might have turned you into a potato or a chicken with my upside-down magic. But thank you, for everything," I said, and she smiled, revealing her white teeth. She tucked her dark hair behind her ears and she only did that whenever she was serious.

"Are you going to keep thanking us or are we going to summon Lord Ravin?" she asked, and I laughed. The fact that they were opposed to the idea of breaching the underworld before my nap, and were now interested in helping me summon him made me happy. I truly hoped I wasn't making a terrible mistake. My transgressions were piling up and eventually, I would pay for them. Hopefully, that wouldn't be with Chloe's life.

"Let's do this," I said, and reached for the Book of Lost Shadows on the center table. Just like the time I used it in summoning Sinn, there was a strange surge of dark power. It loomed around us like a beacon or a warning. I noticed Sinn's face harden. He wasn't confident in my ability to use the book, and I couldn't discount his concerns. I had summoned him accidentally, after all. I opened the Book of Lost Shadows and immediately, the pages opened by themselves, stopping at a page with a step-by-step guide to summoning a being or an object into the human world.

"Did it just read your mind?" Linda asked, and I was too fascinated to respond. The book was undoubtedly powerful, but this was a risky decision to make. No one was truly in control of this kind of power, yet my mother had never let it corrupt her. I had to have confidence that I was as strong as her. I nodded to Linda and Sinn, indicating that I was ready to start.

"We'll need candles and the ash from the box in the attic. The other box," I said and looked at Sinn, knowing he understood the one I meant.

"How do I know the right ash to bring down here?" he asked, looking at me and I concentrated on the Book of Lost Shadows once again.

"The small handwritten instructions on the top right corner, are my mom's notes. It says candles and ash. There are no specifics. Just grab every bottle of ash you can find," I said, and Sinn stood before walking to the stairs, leaving Linda and me alone.

"Is that all we need to summon, Lord Ravin?" Linda asked, and I glanced at the book.

"We just need a drop of my blood. Then we would need to draw the Triquetra, using the ash. Then, we say the spell as many times as possible before Lord Ravin appears."

"Is there any caveat? Something we should worry about?" she asked, and I shrugged. The Book of Lost Shadows didn't mention any negative side effects, but that didn't mean there weren't any. I was out of options and didn't want to think about the dangers of my actions.

"Found it!" Sinn said and raced down the carpeted steps towards us.

"How many bottles of ash?" I asked, and he raised just one. It had no label on it and I wondered if Sinn got the right item.

"I have a strong sense of smell. I gave it a good whiff and confirmed that it was ash before bringing it," he added.

"The candles?" I asked, and he brought two big candles from his back pocket.

"I needed my hands to climb down the pull-down steps. So, I had to improvise. What else do you need?" he asked, passing me the candles.

"We need to draw a Triquetra," Linda announced, and took the bottle from Sinn's hands. Immediately, she moved to the free space separating the center table and the sofa closer to the laundry door. The Triquetra was like a flower with three petals. I reread the spell from the book as she drew it perfectly, using the ash in the bottle.

"What's next?" she asked as she finished, breathing heavily, and I moved into the center of the Triquetra, placing a candle in the middle and on the edge of each petal. I lit them and stepped out of the Triquetra.

"What should I do?" Sinn asked, and I glanced at him for a moment. Then remembered the warnings he shared earlier and decided on the perfect job for him.

"What do we do when something else appears instead of Lord Ravin? Perhaps something hostile?" I asked, and Sinn looked confused for a moment.

"We run?" Linda said, and I chuckled. While that was the reasonable thing to do, I wasn't going to abandon my house, at least not without a fight.

"I suppose that's an option. But I won't let a demon take my home from me. What we will do is fight and send it back," I said with a lighthearted smile that wasn't returned. "That would be your job, Sinn," I added as he frowned.

"What?"

"Your job is to stay on guard and watch our backs. If the Dark God realizes we are doing this and sends one of his minions after us, we need someone who is used to dealing with demons. You were pretty effective at fighting the sphinx." I said, pleased with my backup plan.

Sinn sighed and took a step backward. He was less enthused with his role in my plan than I was. "That's far enough. I feel safer if you are close to me," I said, in a teasing manner, but acknowledged it was completely true. Failing wasn't an option, but I was beginning to admit that victory would be bittersweet, as Sinn would be forced to leave. I couldn't think about that now.

"What's next?" Linda asked as I reined in my wandering thoughts.

"I need a knife from the kitchen," I said, tucking my hair behind my ears. Linda nodded and went to the kitchen, returning a minute later with a small paring knife.

"Here it is," she said, and passed the knife to me. They both had their eyes on me, and I didn't wait for Linda to ask what was next.

"We need to seek passage to the underworld. Then, we can call out to Lord Ravin for a conversation," I said, and they both nodded. Quickly, I cut my thumb with the knife and dropped the blood on the three edges of the Triquetra, and I signaled Linda to move toward me. She had more powerful magic, and she was my anchor. I stepped out of the Triquetra, standing on one side. Linda took the cue from my position and stood on the other side. "We must ask to be connected to the underworld. The spell is Ton Ypókosmo, Anazitoúme Koinó," I said and looked at Linda and Sinn too, giving them a smile as I tried to ease the tension in the room. Then I began to chant, and Linda joined me.

"Ton Ypókosmo, Anazitoúme Koinó! Ton Ypókosmo, Anazitoúme Koinó!"

After about ten seconds of chanting the spell, a strange energy suddenly enveloped me. I locked eyes with Linda immediately, and it was obvious that she felt it too. But we didn't stop chanting, we just intensified our chants.

"Ton Ypókosmo, Anazitoúme Koinó! Ton Ypókosmo, Anazitoúme Koinó!"

We shouted again. This time, I chanted at the top of my voice. If there was someone granting permission for our world to be connected to the underworld, he was definitely not getting any rest until I was answered. Then, suddenly, lightning burst forth from the middle of the Triquetra and it formed a ring above our heads. My heart raced, but we didn't stop chanting. Then, a dark cloud appeared in the ring as we continued. It got darker as wind whipped through the living room.

"It is time to summon Lord Ravin!" I shouted at the top of my lungs and Linda nodded again.

"O Lórdos Rávin apokalýpste ton eaftó sas! O Lórdos Rávin apokalýpste ton eaftó sas!" I chanted.

I began to chant the summoning spell for Lord Ravin, and Linda joined me after the first chant. The cloud looming over our heads grew darker as we chanted and the lightning became thunderous, startling me for a moment. It arced above the room, crackling through the rushing wind.

"O Lórdos Rávin apokalýpste ton eaftó sas! O Lórdos Rávin apokalýpste ton eaftó sas!" we chanted.

We continued as I glanced at Sinn, surprised that he was completely calm amidst this chaos. As we continued to chant, the dark cloud and thunder dropped from the ceiling, filling the entire room and making it impossible for me to see Linda or Sinn. I didn't want to be discouraged, and I tried to chant, but I could no longer speak. It was like there was a force holding down my vocal cords. *What have I done?* I thought, trying to continue chanting as I wondered if there was a way to reverse the spell if needed. The weight on my chest increased, and I fought for breath.

"Sinn. Help," I strained to whisper the words as my sternum felt like I had a hundred-pound weight resting on it. After a few seconds with no intervention from Sinn, I realized I was all alone. He couldn't hear me. As I tried to think of a way to avoid my impending death, the dark cloud and lightning disappeared, forcing me to fall to the floor as I tried to catch my breath.

"Who dared to summon me from my slumber? Who risks the fall of the human realm?" A voice boomed, and I glanced up in haste. This time, a big O formed in my mouth. Lord Ravin was in my living room.

CHAPTER 7

"**W**ho dares to summon me from my sleep? Show yourself and speak before I smite thee." His voice was menacing and for a moment, my legs became too heavy to move. I looked around for Sinn and spotted him watching us. *Isn't he supposed to say something?* I asked myself. But the fact that he wasn't coming to my aid meant that I needed to do this myself. Maybe he couldn't interfere. I took a deep breath before facing Lord Ravin. He was a skeleton, wearing a tattered robe, but his bones looked like they had been placed in a forge. They were burnt and dry. The black robe that hung from his frame had holes in it. Was this what he had been wearing when he died? I wondered and looked closely at the holes in his back. They looked tiny, like bullet holes. Only that there were no bullets in ancient times and it was more likely arrowheads. That he could easily turn and see me but didn't, fascinated me. Perhaps he wasn't allowed to look backward, I wondered, and took a deep breath.

"O wise and great one," I started, looking at Linda, who arched an eyebrow at me. Since we were dealing with someone from ancient times, taking a page from the words of William Shakespeare seemed like the best bet.

"How dare you summon me?" Lord Ravin asked as I appeared before him. For a moment I was speechless, but time wasn't something I had in abundance.

"Forgive me, my lord. But I need your help," I said, taking a soft bow.

"Who are you?" he said, hissing as I stared at him. His eye sockets were emitting dark billows of smoke, and I could feel my heartbeat increasing by the second.

"My Lord. I'm Breena Hutchins. A witch. It is happening again, my Lord. The Dark God is about to win the battle against humanity."

"Has my death been in vain? Have the worlds between the humans and the demons merged together?" he asked, and I shook my head instantly.

"Not yet, my Lord. But, without your help, I fear your death will have been in vain," I said, and Lord Ravin shrieked. I shivered and took two steps backward. I glanced at Sinn, who looked like a guard dog, sensing danger, and I was comforted that he was watching out for me.

"The human world and the underworld must not merge. Thou shall not let this happen. I didn't allow these events to transpire in the Kingdom of Bivlar. Thou must not let it happen, now. How did you find me?" he asked in a loud voice as I swallowed the lump in my throat.

"My Lord, we found the scrolls. We know what happened to Baldwin. We still sing songs of your heroics and how you saved mankind. But we don't know how to stop the Dark God from winning. This is why we summoned you, My Lord. Your insight is priceless in our cause," I said and Lord Ravin calmed.

"Has it happened again?" he asked.

"Yes, it has. My daughter, Chloe, has been cursed."

"Has she joined the Gods?" he asked.

"Not yet."

"Then, she can be saved. But, to save her, thou must locate the Dark God's messenger amongst you," his voice boomed in eerie reverence.

I frowned. "My Lord, there is no one connected to the Dark God in our world. The Dark God cursed my daughter from the underworld."

With his eye sockets still smoking, he growled loudly and looked at me. "Never have I heard of the Dark God doing his own bidding. He feels such tasks beneath him. There must be one. A messenger, a person with darkness within, and thou must find that person. Only the messenger could have cursed thy child."

As I tried to ask another question and get more clarity, we heard a loud noise and Lord Ravin hissed, he glanced around as if looking for something we couldn't see. He looked scared, and it was obvious that something was coming to end our connection. Our breach between the worlds was no longer a secret to the rulers of the underworld.

"I must retire. The reaper comes. Find the messenger. The fate of the whole world and the Gods depends on it," he said.

"Wait," I tried to continue, but it was too late. His bones crumbled and became smoke, and it was like he was never there, as everything returned to normal. I looked at Linda and saw that she had broken the Triquetra and that was most likely the reason why Lord Ravin disappeared.

"Why did you do that?" I asked. I was angry, that I didn't get more information from the only person who could help us.

"Didn't you hear him? The reaper was coming. If we let him into our world, even Sinn wouldn't be able to stop him from reaping our souls to the underworld. We aren't going to save the world if we are dead," she said, and cleaned the ashes from the Triquetra. She gathered them in a small circle where the center of the Triquetra used to be, and I hated that she was right. Letting Lord Ravin stay any longer than he did could have been disastrous.

"I'm sorry. You did the right thing. But I don't understand what he meant about the Dark Lord having a messenger in our world," I said as Sinn approached us.

"It's pretty simple. There is someone in this world helping him. A human who is so wicked in heart that it has become a minion for the Dark Lord. This person poisoned your daughter and we need to find out who it is," Sinn said, and sat down. His sense of calm despite the situation was fascinating, considering my heart was still racing like a runaway train.

Linda dusted off her hands. "If this messenger was in contact with Chloe, I could access her recent memories and we could discover who it is. If she didn't see who cursed her, then we will have to discern who would be easily converted by the Dark God. Which of the witches is weak of heart and couldn't fight the temptation of more power?"

"You are sure it's a witch? You realize that means it's someone we trust. Worse, someone Chloe trusted," I said.

Linda nodded. "It has to be a witch or warlock to perform this kind of curse. I'm pretty sure the boost in power would be the temptation for any being of magic. Perhaps more power than the coven combined. Or a chance at immortality when humanity is wiped out for good."

Linda's suggestion made my stomach roll, mostly because I agreed with her assessment. There was a good chance one of our own, betrayed us. We needed to find this messenger. Could we tap into Chloe's memory? Would it make her worse? What if it killed her? What if her connection to the

Dark God alerted him to our plan? The questions continued to roll through my mind yet I couldn't answer any of them.

"Is there anything else we can do?" I asked with a frown.

"I know you are worried for Chloe and you don't want to do anything that could put her in danger. But remember what Lord Ravin said. If we don't find the messenger that cursed Chloe, then it will eventually lead to her death. We have to find the traitor. You realize that we aren't talking about an ordinary human. We are talking about a witch or warlock. One capable of using dark magic. We need to find this person before another daughter or son is cursed. The more people sacrificed to the Dark God, the stronger he becomes," Linda said.

Still, I was worried for Chloe. That my actions would cause her more harm. But what options did I have? Dead if you do or dead if you don't, isn't much of a choice. I found it ironic that finding this traitor was the best chance of saving Chloe. But, could I risk her life to save the world? I knew the answer. I just didn't like it.

"I need something to drink," I said, and strolled to the kitchen. I filled up a glass with milk and downed it in a few loud gulps.

"You need to slow down. You will make yourself sick," I heard as I filled the glass again, and I turned to see Sinn and Linda standing behind me. Their eyes held concern and understanding, but I couldn't take their pity.

"What?" I asked, almost shouting.

"You need to slow down on the milk. You will make yourself sick," Sinn said as I fought the urge to tell him it wasn't the milk making me ill.

"I meant, why are you guys looking at me like that?" I asked again.

Linda sighed. "It's obvious that you are warring with your

conscious. You are weighing your options, and trying to make the right decision. You think this might be like the potion? But it's not. You are also forgetting something important," Linda replied, and I fixed my eyes on her before dropping the glass in the sink and resting my hands on my waist.

"And what is that?" I asked.

"You have us. We wouldn't do anything to harm Chloe. She is the reason we are doing all this. We would never endanger her on purpose. Think about the alternatives. Do you want us to go from house to house and inquire about witches with a connection to dark magic? No witch would admit to that, or the coven would imprison them. We would only succeed in spooking our traitor, making it more difficult to ferret them out. We need to tap into Chloe's memories before she became unconscious," Linda said.

"We won't do anything without your permission and we have lost the luxury of time," Sinn added.

I hated dilemmas and the way they always made me feel. There appeared to be no right answer, only the lesser of two evils. Once again, my daughter's life was held in the balance of my decision. Sadly, they were right. I didn't have much of a choice.

"Fine. Let's tap into her memories. But, as soon as it becomes dangerous, you have to stop everything and I mean it," I said, looking at Linda sternly and she gave a soft nod.

"I wouldn't do anything to hurt Chloe. She is like a daughter to me," Linda said. That was true, but it held little comfort. My skin crawled with fear that I had made a wrong choice, but there was no going back. We would spell my daughter and hope for the best.

"What do you need?" I asked, as Linda winked at me and placed her hands on her chest, making downward motions with them. She wanted me to be calm. Was there a mother on earth that would be calm in this situation? I doubted it.

"I don't need any ingredients. I have had the spells for memory recollection since I was a teenager. Chloe is safe, but you should be by my side. It would mean a lot to have a witch supporting me in this," she said. There was no way I would have let Linda do the spell alone, but I appreciated her including me, all the same.

"Well, this witch has upside-down magic. But, it seems you need some unpredictable witch support. We have to do something that the Dark God wouldn't expect, remember?"

"Just don't give your daughter a second head," Linda said.

"I'm leaving the chanting to you, then. We will just be there to support you," I said, looking at Sinn and it took him some seconds to respond.

"Y—yes. We will be there," he replied quickly.

"What are we waiting for? Let's find whatever is in Chloe's mind," Linda said and led the way to Chloe's bedroom. I should be happy for the chance to discover who was helping the Dark God, but I was filled with apprehension as I walked past the kitchen doors. I was scared of what we would discover.

CHAPTER 8

I followed Linda up the stairs with Sinn behind me. This was it. There was no turning back now. "Nothing will happen to her. Trust me," Linda said as she entered Chloe's room. The faint smell of lavender pot-pourri drifted from the opening, and I recognized the blend of soothing herbs. Linda had brought them often when I was dealing with Marcellus' death. I trusted Linda, but this was my decision and I wouldn't be able to live with myself if anything happened to my daughter.

Linda walked towards Chloe, sitting at the edge of the bed, by her chest, so she could hold the sides of Chloe's head in her hands easily. I took a seat by the edge of the bed, by Chloe's legs, watching as Linda closed her eyes and focused on Chloe's mind. I had seen her perform the spell before, but had never experienced it myself.

"Apokálypsé mou, o Mnimosýni. Apokálypse mou to periechómeno sto myaló tis!" Linda said, loudly.

She chanted again as Sinn stood behind me and placed his hands on my shoulders, giving them a gentle squeeze. His hands made me less tense, but my heart raced and I couldn't respond.

"Apokálypsé mou, o Mnimosýni. Apokálypse mou to periechómeno sto myaló tis!" Linda chanted again, and I prayed in silence. She was calling on Mnemosyne, the goddess of memory, asking for access into Chloe's mind. But I feared it might not be enough, especially when the host was cursed by a Dark god. Was the goddess stronger than the Dark god? Only time would tell.

She chanted for the third time, and Chloe's body jerked forward, startling me. Her chest arced off the bed, then slumped back.

"She moved. That's a good sign, right?" I asked, standing up. It was a dream come true that my daughter moved after so long of lying motionless and unconscious. Linda looked at me, but she didn't say anything. With her hands still on Chloe's head, she chanted again.

"Apokálypsé mou, o Mnimosýni. Apokálypse mou to periechómeno sto myaló tis!"

Immediately after the last word left Linda's lips, a white light streamed from Chloe's eyes into Linda's eyes. They leaned closer to one another, and I knew it was working. Linda was in Chloe's mind.

"Are there any dangers to this procedure?" Sinn asked.

"Normally I would say no, but there is a chance Linda could be overwhelmed by the Dark God's power. This could anchor her in Chloe's mind and make it impossible to bring her out. So, yeah, there is something to worry about," I said and Sinn's jaw dropped.

"Why did you let her do this when there is a chance of her getting stuck in Chloe's mind forever?"

"Not forever. Only until Chloe dies. Which in turn could

kill Linda. Before you get uppity, remember that you supported this idea," I said.

"That's because I didn't know the risks involved," Sinn shot back, and I sighed.

"Linda knew the risks too. She's a fighter. She would bring a war to the Dark God if he tries to trap her. Don't worry. Linda knows what she is doing," I said. But it was obvious that Sinn wasn't as convinced as I was. "Calm down," I added, and stood to meet him as he paced in the bedroom. "You need to stop, Sinn."

"How long can she remain like that?" he asked, and I held his hand, stopping him from walking away from me.

"It could be a minute or for a few hours. We can't say, we aren't in Chloe's mind and we can't help her," I said, matching his gaze. "She's safe," I added., and pulled him in for a hug, holding him tightly. After a few seconds, he wrapped his hands around me and took a deep breath. "Nothing will happen to her," I repeated just as Linda jerked suddenly and emerged from the trance.

"I told you she was safe," I said, rushing to Linda's side. I knelt before her.

"Linda, are you okay?" I asked, holding her head with my hands as she panicked. Whatever she saw in Chloe's mind had traumatized her, and sweat beaded my brow as I waited for Linda to settle her breathing. "Take deep breaths," I ordered her, and she took a deep breath, then another.

"I—I—I know who the messenger of the Dark God is in Drima Falls. I know who placed the Dark God's curse on Chloe," she said between deep breaths, and I held her head firmly with my hand.

"Stop talking now. Take a minute to anchor your mind in our reality. You are safe," I said and looked at Sinn. "I need a glass of water," I whispered to him, and he dashed out of the bedroom.

"There is an enemy amongst us. We had an enemy living amongst us the whole time. We need to get her. She must not escape," she said, beginning to panic again, and I wrapped my hands around her.

"Shhhh… stop talking and just breathe."

A few seconds later, Sinn walked in with a glass full of water. I mouthed thank you before taking it from him. Quickly, I passed the water to Linda. "Drink up." She drank the water, returning the glass to me when it was empty. I set it on the floor beside me and turned to face her. Linda's color was returning, and I rubbed her leg as she settled.

"Now, take your time. Tell me what you saw," I said softly, and Linda nodded.

"There was a lot of information to deal with in her mind. After surfing through the barrage of images, I focused on her memories of the day she became unconscious and… and… I saw it. The messenger. For the curse to work, the Dark God's messenger needed to ensure that Chloe had a high concentration of witch energy. Her essence had to be pure. She needed to be around her, close to her, like a mother or friend would be."

"These clues will make me mad if you don't tell me who it is." I was getting impatient.

"Who would be closer to Chloe than you? Or me? Who had unrestricted access to your daughter?" She asked instead of telling me, and I frowned. I gave her questions a thought and there was no answer on my mind. I had no idea.

"I doubt there is anyone as close as we are to Chloe. No one has that kind of access. Not even her teacher in high school, and she didn't do this. She isn't a witch." I finally said.

Linda frowned at me and I considered my daughter's social interactions. Chloe was a reserved child. She didn't have many friends at school or at home. Her life was almost militant in its routine, and I always knew where she was at any given moment. Apart from school, work, and her home life, the only time she left the house was for her mentorship under the elder witch Ravana Victious. Then my eyes widened in shock.

"It can't be. Tell me I'm wrong. This cannot be the work of Ravana Victious! It can't be!" I shouted, and Linda said nothing for a moment, confirming my shock.

"She is the closest thing to a mother other than me and she played on that trust. She got close and used Chloe to evoke the curse. The day she came to visit was to confirm that it worked and when we gave excuses for Chloe, she knew it had. She is the devil, Linda. We have been living a lie, and she has the coven's trust," I said, feeling the guilt overwhelm me. It was my fault for allowing Chloe to apprentice with Ravana in order to become a better witch. I couldn't teach her. My magic made me more of a liability than an asset to my only daughter.

"I shouldn't have listened to Ravana when she came and offered her help. I was so embarrassed about my failing magic and it's about to cost me my daughter's life. My vanity has put my only child in danger. I practically handed her to the Dark God," I said, and Sinn, who had been silent, walked to me, stopping just in front of me. I allowed the tears that filled my eyes to fall.

"It's not your fault, and the battle isn't over yet," Sinn said, and he released my arms, holding my hands before they fell to the side.

"You were just looking out for Chloe's interests. Trying to make the best decision for your child. She should have been safe with Ravana. She is an elder witch and a trusted member of the coven. I would have accepted her offer as well. Don't be too hard on yourself. She has fooled everyone in Drima Falls." His voice was calm and reassuring.

As much as I wanted to believe that it wasn't my fault, I couldn't help it. I couldn't forgive myself for putting my only child in this situation. I knew Ravana didn't like me. She and Marcellus had been friends since they were children and she never thought I was good enough for him, but she seemed to adore Chloe. How could I be so stupid?

"You also lost Marcellus during that time. Emotionally, you weren't at your best. You can't blame yourself for something none of us saw. If Ravana hadn't turned to dark magic and sought more power, we wouldn't be having this conversation," she said, and Sinn hugged me. It was unexpected, but it was what I needed.

"I didn't protect Chloe. No matter the circumstances, that is the truth," I cried out, loud enough for the neighbors to hear my sobs. I looked at Chloe and she had returned to her immobile state.

"It's not your fault. Not at all," Linda said in a reassuring tone.

"Instead of focusing on events beyond our control, let's work on a solution. How do we save Chloe? How do we find Ravana? What do we need this dark witch to do in order to break the curse?" Sinn asked, and I glanced at Chloe for a moment. He was right. While Ravana's betrayal cut deep, we did know who the messenger was.

I did what every mother would do. I ran toward the door.

CHAPTER 9

"Where do you think you are going to?" Sinn asked and blocked me before I got to the door. He moved so fast I bumped into him, but I was too pissed to praise his speed.

"Where do you think?" I shot back, breathing heavily. Linda patted Chloe's hand, then walked over to us. "Why are we wasting time here while our enemy is stalking Drima Falls? Why are you trying to stop me when you should be helping me? Don't you want to end this?" I asked as they glanced at each other.

"Get out of my way," I said and tried to walk past him, but Sinn moved his body to the door, blocking it.

"You aren't going out like this. You are pissed and you are not thinking straight. You aren't likely to make an informed decision," Sinn said, and I shook my head. This wasn't a decision. It was a necessity and the only move we had.

"You guys, stopping me is the wrong decision." I wasn't going to back down, and I let my anger show.

Linda sighed. "Answer me this. I know you are going to

Ravana Victious' home. So, tell me what your plan is once you get there."

"It's simple. I'm going to ask her why she did what she did. How she could betray Chloe and the coven's trust," I said angrily as this little talk was delaying us from stopping the messenger of the Dark God.

"So, you expect Ravana, an elder witch, and who we just found out is the messenger of the Dark God, to just confess to you? That she would be forthcoming with that information when she has hidden it so well?"

"Yes, I will warn her that she can't go against the coven alone and if she puts an end to all this, I will keep my mouth shut and she can live her life for as long as it doesn't affect mine or Chloe's."

Sinn huffed. "Oh please. That will never happen. She is powerful and seeks more. She isn't going to be afraid of a witch with little magic."

His words stung, and I knew he meant them, too. Not to hurt me, but to make me see reason. I could see his point. I just didn't want to back down. Any chance to save Chloe was worth taking. "She was reasonable once. Maybe she can be again. I only want to talk to her. But if she wants to fight, then she's about to find out what I am willing to do to save my daughter."

"What you are willing to do? Are you even listening to yourself?" Linda asked, placing her hands on her hips. She was mad, but I was livid and desperate. It was obvious that they were united against me, and I wasn't going to win this argument. "She would snap your neck without breaking a sweat. Your magic is faulty, remember? Even when it's at full power, you are no match for an elder witch. If you were, then you would be a council member, not Ravana. The council has wanted to replace her for years, but she is too powerful."

"I realize that…"

Linda held up a hand. "Let me finish. For all we know, she had been fortifying her dark power in preparation for this war. She is the Dark God's messenger. We have no idea what abilities she has gained. If you go alone, you could die."

"Then what would you have me do?" I snapped back, frustrated by the never-ending reminder that I was weak and couldn't protect my daughter. "I can't sit here and cry when the person who did all this is out there, looking for her next victim. It's only a matter of time before another daughter falls prey to the Dark God."

"We are trying to stop you from going on a suicide mission. But we never said we wouldn't do anything about it," Linda said, glancing at Sinn. It was obvious that he had no idea what she was talking about.

"It seems you are the only one with information on how to stop Ravana. Sinn doesn't look like he is on the same page with you," I said.

"It just caught me off guard. I wouldn't allow you to leave this house to face a woman who is more powerful than you. You are letting your frustration get to you. I understand, but we need a plan, not a retaliatory move, that ends in Chloe's death."

I knew he was right, but not retaliating was hard, and I wondered if they were trying to make me feel better or they meant what they said. "So, we are all going together?" I asked, praying I understood them correctly.

"Let's get this done. I'm famished too. Perhaps we can get something to eat on the way back," Linda said, and walked to the door. Sinn moved, and I glanced at Chloe for some seconds. "I will save you, even if it is the last thing I do," I whispered, and Sinn placed his hands on my shoulder, guiding me out of Chloe's bedroom.

"Are we going to think about this all day or are we going to pay Ravana Victious a visit?" Linda shouted from the living room, and I ran the remaining length of the carpeted steps to the living room.

"Let's go," I said and walked to the front door. Sinn joined me, with Linda behind him. I had no idea what would happen if we visited Ravana, but there was no stopping now. We head outside to my Carolla together.

Ravana's residence sat on ten acres of land on the outskirts of Drima Falls. There were no other houses on the property, and it was eerily silent as they approached. "Why does she live here?" Sinn asked as the Toyota Corolla turned down the dirt road leading to the mansion. There were no gates before the three-story house. I assumed that Ravana trusted her powers to protect the house from intruders and thieves.

As the mansion came into full view, I began to have mixed feelings about what we were about to do. For the first time since I found out that Ravana was a traitor, I wondered if this was a trap. She knew about Linda's abilities. Surely, she would suspect we would check Chloe's memories, eventually. Would we be facing more than a dark witch at Ravana's home?

The exterior of the house had purple mimosa trees growing around it. Petals and tree branches littered the ground, and it looked like she hadn't hired a gardener in a long time. The circular turnaround before the white mansion was overgrown and brown stains rain down the mortal exterior. The dragon statue in the center of the driveway had spit a stream of crystal-clear water, but it now sat in a stagnant pool of green algae. The last time I was here was before Marcellus' death and the grounds had been pristine. I barely recognized them now.

The car came to a halt in front of the main door. The white roman columns sat like sentries at the front, but the dark smudges made them look like they were rotting. I got out of the driver's side, surveying the area. The pavement leading to the front door was cracked, and the house looked like it hadn't been lived in for months.

"Are you sure there is anyone living here?" Sinn asked as he took note of the environment. I couldn't answer and began to wonder if Ravana had another residential address.

"We can keep guessing or we can knock on her door and find out if she is here," Linda said, walking to the front entrance.

"Wait!" I called out, but she ignored me. She placed her knuckles on the door and as she tried to knock, the door opened by itself. We froze as Linda leaned into the house, looking into the front room.

"Ravana is smart. This door doesn't open to humans, just witches," she said as she peered in. I doubted that Ravana would want just anyone to have access to her home, and my internal alarm chimed. Linda glanced at me then pointed to the door. "Watch this," she said, and took two steps backward. Immediately, the door closed. "Sinn, try opening the door," she ordered, and Sinn looked at us for a moment.

"Are you sure about this?" he asked, and I nodded, knowing we wouldn't be getting into the house until Linda had proved her point or failed.

"Get on with it," I said quickly, and Sinn sighed as he walked closer to the door. He stood in front of it, took a deep breath, and knocked on the door. This time, it didn't open, and Linda matched my gaze.

"I told you... it's just for witches. Sinn, try turning the

doorknob to see if the door will open." Upon Linda's order, Sinn held the doorknob and turned it clockwise. It didn't open, and he turned it anti-clockwise, still, it didn't open.

"Fine, you have proved your point. Can we find Ravana, now?" I asked, as my voice cracked with frustration. The longer we waited, the higher our chances of failure. I wondered if Ravana knew we were here as Linda led the way into the house. I was expecting to enter the living room as I walked into the house, but the floor plan had changed. When had she renovated?

Instead, we entered a long corridor. It had several doors on either side, and they were all streaked with green algae. Why renovate with this strange floor plan and then let the place rot? The light fixtures mounted on the walls were the same shell-shaped sconces Ravana had before. There were just more of them, though none were lit. Everything about this new floor plan seemed off.

"I think we should split up to cover more ground," Linda said after glancing at the doors.

I shook my head. "We aren't splitting up. I've seen enough scary movies to know splitting up is a bad idea. Everywhere we go, we go together."

Linda frowned. "Come on, we can cover more ground if we split up. Besides, I'm still a witch, and I'm pretty sure Ravana can't kill me before you guys come to my rescue. You can go with Sinn. He will protect you."

"We. Are. Not. Splitting. Up!" I said, stressing each word. I turned to Sinn, looking to him to back me up.

"I know you want us to cover more ground, but I agree with Bree. It's safer if we stay together," he said, and I breathed a sigh of relief.

"Well, I didn't expect you to go against the witch who summoned you," Linda said with her arms crossed.

"It's not about that. You might be able to fight Ravana. We know she is the Dark God's messenger, but she may have other help. What if she isn't alone?" Sinn asked and Linda couldn't answer. Unless she wanted to lie to herself, she knew Sinn was right, and I wasn't ready to lose another person I loved.

"Fine… let's just get this over with," she said and walked to the first door before we could discuss a strategy or if this was an ambush. Linda touched the first hallway door, and it opened by itself. She looked at me, giving me the 'I told you so' look, and I suppressed a laugh, looking around cautiously. There was no furniture, only an eclectic array of figurines, toys, and pictures. The room was painted a dark blue and every item in the room was a similar dark color. While eerie, with the contents chosen by color and not by style or relevance, the room was at least clean. Still, there was no sign of Ravana.

"We don't need to waste time in this room, she isn't here," I said and walked towards the door as Linda picked up a blue carousel figurine that sat on a royal blue trunk.

"Why color code a room?" Linda asked, replacing the carousel.

"Let's go to the next one," I said in a serious tone. I walked from the room and caught a glimpse of movement at the end of the corridor. But when I turned towards it, there was nothing. Not even the black curtain hanging at the sides of the lone window at the end.

"What's wrong? Did you see something?" Sinn asked as he reached my side and, I assumed, I imagined it.

"Nothing… I didn't see anything. I am being paranoid," I said, not wanting to admit I was letting my frustration get to me.

We walked into the room opposite of the blue one and

were accosted by a fetid odor. It smelled like swamp gas and rotting meat. With no windows, and no light switch by the door, we couldn't make out anything in the room.

Linda put her hand over her mouth and nose. "Dear lord. What is that?"

"We need light," I said as I tried to figure out what was causing the foul odor. Linda brought out her phone and turned on the light. She shone it into the room, and we all gasped. In the middle of the room was a large oak table big, but instead of place settings was a massive decaying deer. The antlers hung off the table as black blood dried on the floor beneath.

"Why would you leave the body of a deer here after getting what you want from the body? That is disgusting," Linda said, and walked out of the room. I glanced at the dead deer and could no longer stand the smell. I exited the room, with Sinn following me. Linda paced in the corridor and I stopped before her, placing my hands on her shoulders.

"Why don't you use a location spell? Can't you find Ravana with one?" Sinn asked, and my eyes lit up.

"Why didn't we think about that?" I asked, and Linda nodded.

"I can do it. But I need something that represents Ravana."

"Where can we find that?" I asked, looking around for clues, but the hall was empty and I wasn't eager to explore the other rooms.

"We need to search each room until we find something that will work. What do you need?" Sinn asked, and I turned to Linda.

"Anything personal. A picture… a piece of jewelry… her hair… anything that represents her," Linda said, and I nodded.

"Let's do this quickly," I said, and we ran to the second

door on the left. It was empty, with black painted walls, and I wondered why she chose that color. Was it necessary when you turned to dark magic? Or a plan to scare off visitors? I had no idea, and there was no time to waste. Four more doors and we came into a room that had a rocking chair and a fireplace that was still burning. It looked like this was where Ravana relaxed. While it was the only room to have a cozy feel, neither the chair nor fireplace was personal. There wasn't even a mantle or a picture on the wall.

"Found it!" Sinn said, and I turned to see him standing by the chair. I walked to him and saw a picture in his hands. It was a passport of Ravana. She looked younger and more beautiful and I wondered why it was there. "It was just lying on the chair," he said, and I couldn't help but feel it was too easy to find.

"We have a witch to locate," Linda said, and took the picture from Sinn's hands. I angled my body to focus on her as she mouthed the spell. "**Deíxe mou poion thélo.**" Which meant show me whom I seek. Then, a bright light, the size of a pearl, appeared before Linda and began to move.

"Follow me," Linda said, and walked from the room. I followed her, with Sinn beside me. The light bead lit the corridor and my heart beat faster as it led us down the hallway. We passed several more doors, and I was thankful we didn't need to inspect them.

If Ravana Victious was in this house, there was no way she didn't know we were here and that we weren't friendly. We followed the light in silence, and I looked around, taking note of my environment.

The light got to the last door at the end of the corridor, on the right, and Linda turned to face us.

"According to the spell, Ravana is in here," she whispered, and I nodded. Why would she sit in there when she knew we would check all doors? I wondered, but there was no time to think about the dark witch's motives.

I walked to the door and turned the doorknob. The door opened and again, it was a dark room with black walls. When a foul smell hit me, I covered my mouth. "Not again. Is there another dead animal? What is it this time?" I asked, and Linda shrugged. Linda took her phone's light and flashed it into the room, but it was empty.

Stunned, I took a step further into the room and the foul smell got stronger. Where was this rotten odor coming from? The empty room made me curious, and I couldn't discern any reason for the smell. Then, a dark power enveloped me. It was different from the energy emitted by the Book of Lost Shadows. But it was similar to the energy I felt when Lord Ravin was scared of the Reaper in my living room.

"There's something here. Something is in here with us. I think Ravana just tricked us." I turned to Linda and Sinn, and their eyes were on me.

"We are in danger. Don't you feel that?"

"There is nothing here," Linda said, looking over the room with her light. I wondered why she wasn't feeling what I did. Her magic was far stronger than mine.

"You seriously don't feel that?" I asked, and Linda shook her head.

"I felt some weird kind of dark energy when Lord Ravin was scared of the Reaper, and I'm getting that same feeling right now. There's something here, and it has malevolent intent. This was Ravana's plan. She knew we would try to locate her and used a cloning spell. But she didn't send us to the wrong place. She just put us some hours behind her to send us to our death."

"Death? But there is nothing here," Sinn said, and

immediately, the dark energy passed through my body, towards the door.

"What?" Linda asked, and I shrugged.

"I don't know. The energy has dissipated. Perhaps I'm being over paranoid," I said, and turned to face Linda. We heard a loud shriek and our attention turned to the door.

CHAPTER 10

My heart squeezed and for a moment it felt like my soul was being leeched from my body. "What's that?" I asked, clutching my chest. As if my white knuckles could somehow keep me alive. I saw nothing, but every nerve ending screamed that I was in imminent danger.

"I don't know. I've never heard anything like that before," Linda said, but Sinn's eyes darted around the room before focusing on the door. They flashed red, and I wondered if his demon side saw something oblivious to us.

Then, he looked at us and said, "Run!"

"What?" I asked, looking around. He remained focused on something only he could see. "What did you see?" I asked, again and Sinn pushed me toward the door.

"Run. Now. Don't look back," he said in a stern voice, and as I ran toward the door, Sinn stopped me, holding my hand. "Not that way," he said, and I glanced toward the door as a form began to appear. We froze, but it was like our legs were too heavy to move. My eyes widened in fear when eight huge legs clicked against the floor. They were black with sharp claw tips at the end. The form began to solidify, and I found it hard to swallow my spit. It was a creature with the body of a giant spider and the head of an angry bull, and I wished I had listened to Sinn in the beginning and rushed outside before the thing had appeared.

"What's that? I asked, taking a few steps backward as Linda followed.

"That's a Gracko, another minion of the Dark God. And yes, this creature is stronger than a sphinx," Sinn said as I wondered how he could be so calm in a situation like this. The creature shrieked again and I felt my soul shudder as if the sound was weakening it.

"Let's run," I said, and turned. But, we appeared to be in a different house. There were no doors to the left or right anymore, and we were in one large hallway without pictures or windows. When I thought the situation couldn't get any stranger, the hallway began to move, getting bigger and smaller, then twisting like an accordion. Sinn pulled me closer to him as he watched the creature.

"We are in a maze," Sinn said, and while my mind raced as to how we got there and how Ravana summoned this monster, one thing was for sure. We were in Ravana's circus, and she was in control of the show.

The creature shrieked again, stomping its claws into the ground before it charged at us. For a demon with the head of a bull, its spider legs scurried unbelievably fast. In seconds, it was within striking distance, and it shot a flying web from a forward leg. "Watch out!" Sinn shouted and pushed me out of the way of a string of web hurtling toward me. I looked back at the web as it hit the wall behind me and it created a little hole in the concrete. Any blow would be fatal, but how did we avoid the strings of death in a cramped space like this?

"Linda? Can you make a shield, and buy us some time?" I asked, cursing under my breath. I felt useless with my magic on the fritz and being forced to rely on Linda. She mouthed a spell and a blue iridescent shield formed between them and the creature.

"It won't hold for long!" she shouted, and I nodded.

"How do we kill this thing? Does it have a weakness?" I asked, and Sinn shook his head.

"This is the first time I've encountered a Gracko, but legend says they are indestructible," Sinn said. We had more problems than solutions and it was beginning to piss me off. I turned toward the demon. It had begun to strike the shield. Each thunderous smash of its spiked claw tip, cracked the blue iridescent shield Linda created. It was obvious by the sound of shattering glass that he would be upon us soon. Whatever Ravana had done to relocate us, we were in the Gracko's domain and he wasn't happy about it.

Linda leaned toward me. "I don't know if this helps, but I read a scientific study that the only weak points in a spider are the legs, joints, and the mouth," Linda said as my hands became sweaty. I appraised the creature's body, looking for any weakness. It was a few deafening blows away from the shield breaking.

Sinn glanced at Linda. "If the scientific study about a spider's weak points is our only option, I suggest we try it out. I will distract the Gracko and whatever happens, stay back. Linda, you prepare a death spell. It will only work if the Gracko's mouth is open. When I give the call, Linda, perform the spell. Our timing needs to be perfect and remember, don't try to help me," Sinn said in a stern voice.

The creature growled and launched a series of rapid attacks on the shield. The cracking and tinkling of glass alerted us that he would be breaking through it very soon.

"What if his mouth isn't a weak spot?" I asked. It had been a while since I was worried about a man and I realized I didn't want to lose Sinn like I did Marcellus. I couldn't go through that again. Somehow in the short time we had spent together, he had become an integral part of my life.

"Then we die," Sinn said and my heart stuttered. Before I could reply, the creature broke through the shield, shrieking its victory as it lunged at us. Sinn moved away from Linda and effectively taking the Gracko's attention with him. He ran toward the creature. As he got close, his demon side emerged, the one I saw when we went into the magical painting. His red eyes and angular features had freaked the shit out of me. But this time, I wasn't scared that Sinn was a demon. He looked more like my demon prince in shiny armor. Only he wasn't returning from a victory at war, but was pursuing a battle where death looked more certain than victory.

"He's going to die, Linda," I called out as he took a blow from the creature and was sent flying hard into the left wall. His body was imprinted in the gyp rock when he fell to the floor. Sinn jumped to his feet and charged the Gracko again. My jaw hurt from clenching my teeth together. The fear of watching, wishing, and praying that he didn't get thrown into another wall or worse was excruciating. My heart leapt when Sinn landed a blow to the creature's head. It was directly on the forehead and this sent the Gracko backward and onto his back.

"Yesssss! Finish him, Sinn!" I shouted like a cheerleader giving support to a basketball team. Sinn took my advice and rushed at the creature, who was trying to flip himself over. Sinn grabbed one of the legs and broke it from its joints, throwing it to the ground. The Gracko shrieked loudly before it turned over successfully, looking at Sinn with death in its eyes.

Sinn grabbed the severed leg, waving it before the creature, laughing in a deep scary voice and the creature shrieked again. As the loud deafening noise ended, a new leg reformed where the severed one used to be. Sinn hissed and took a few steps back.

"Great! A monster with the power to regenerate its limbs. What other surprises do you have for us, Ravana?" I shouted, as if she was listening. My frustration grew when I noticed Sinn had black blood trickling down his arms. He was injured. Had the initial blow had a more severe effect on him than I thought? I didn't want to think about the number of blows his demon side could handle before he became human again. Was he stronger as a demigod, or was the curse affecting him?

Sinn took two steps backward and glanced at me. I expected to find fear or concern on his face and red eyes, but a smile formed and he laughed louder than normal. "What are you trying to do? You will only enrage the creature more!" I shouted. As if the Gracko was listening to what I said, fire came out of its nostrils and it charged at Sinn. The speed was faster than before and I feared the blow would be fatal.

Sinn didn't run after the creature like before. "Run!" I said and tried to move closer to him, but Linda held me tightly.

"He said we shouldn't help," Linda said.

I looked at Sinn as the first blow came. It landed around the rib cage and I gasped as Sinn coughed out blood. I heard his ribs crack. The echo ripped through my soul. I feared the blow was fatal when Sinn staggered to the side, unable to stand up straight. He bent to the side where the blow landed and my heart beat faster when his face was etched in pain.

"I will enjoy killing you," the creature said, shrieking its triumph.

"It can talk? Like a human? Just when I thought this couldn't get any weirder," I said to Linda who was surprisingly calm, watching Sinn evade the creature's blows. I whimpered when another blow landed on Sinn's side, and he howled in pain.

"Sinn… come back. That thing is too strong!" I shouted loud enough for him to hear, but he ignored my call. He growled before he lunged at the Gracko. "Noooooo!" I screamed as the creature thrust a thick black leg toward Sinn's neck. The blow would have been fatal, but Sinn ducked and rolled under the creature, evading the attack. I took a deep breath as he landed a low on the Gracko's stomach, causing it to shriek again.

"Linda, help him," I said as tears welled in my eyes, but she didn't respond. "Linda!" I called out again, and she looked at me sharply.

"Sinn said we should wait. Helping him could put him in more danger. And don't even think about using magic. With your luck you would turn Sinn into an ant or a hamster," she said, and returned her gaze to the battle as I scowled in frustration.

Sinn charged again and as he tried to dodge the creature's dagger-like claw, it adjusted its attack, catching Sinn's torso and sending him hard to the ground. He rolled away, but he left a trail of blood behind him.

"Sinn! Get up! Please! You aren't dying on me," I said as tears rolled down my cheeks. Sinn tried to stand, but after several attempts that landed him on his back, it was obvious he couldn't. He appeared unconscious as he lay completely still, and I knew we would all be Gracko food soon. I hissed my anger at the minion of the Dark God and another win for Ravana. The creature stood over Sinn's almost lifeless body and shrieked its victory. It opened its mouth, which revealed sharp fangs. As it leaned closer for the death blow, Sinn reared up and grabbed its mouth, holding its jaw open with all his strength.

"Linda! Now!" he shouted, and I glanced at Linda as she began the death spell. The easiest, yet most powerful spell to end the life of any target it encountered. I held my breath as Sinn fought with the creature. It tried to pull away from his deadly embrace by sending blow after blow into Sinn's upper and lower body. Our window of opportunity was beginning to close when Sinn coughed up blood.

"Linda! Hurry!" I shouted, and she sped up the spell, taking slow steps towards the combatants. It was crucial for the death spell to hit the creature and not Sinn, and I said a silent prayer to whatever God was listening as she unleashed the spell into the open mouth. Sinn released the Gracko and jumped out of the way, just in time. The spell entered the mouth of the Gracko and the creature took several steps backward. Another large shriek broke out as steam rose from its nostrils. It shook violently, as if it was in an earthquake before it disintegrated in a puff of black ash.

I rushed to Sinn, who had fallen to the ground like a broken branch. "Sinn! Stay with me!" I shouted and propped his head into my lap.

"It worked," he said and smiled, coughing out blood again.

"Yes, it did. Let's never do that again, though. My heart can't take it," I said. I traced my fingers over his bruised ribs, and he groaned in pain.

"We didn't die. But it will be harder to find Ravana now," Sinn said, and I smoothed back his hair. His demon side was strangely comforting, and the red eyes now added to his sex appeal. Not that he needed more of that. I smiled as he resumed his human form. The injuries remained, and Linda knelt beside me, inspecting his wounds.

"Let's help him up," I said, and she moved to Sinn's left side, supporting his weight as I took the right. The house had returned to normal, and we left the room, returning to the hallway like nothing had happened. We had failed again. It wasn't going to be easy to find the Dark God's messenger.

We walked slowly through the corridor, taking one slow step at a time. Each caused Sinn to groan in pain. He coughed up blood again, and I wondered if he was bleeding internally.

"Do we need to get to the hospital?" I said, looking at Sinn as Linda reached out and opened the front door.

"It is not necessary to visit the hospital. I just need to rest. Let's go home," Sinn said, groaning again, but I wasn't convinced.

"What do you do when you are injured as a demon?" I asked as we escorted Sinn to the Corolla. Linda opened the car door for Sinn and we settled him into the back seat.

"I rest and heal," he replied, groaning again.

"What—," as I tried to talk, Linda shot me a 'shut up' look and I bit my lip to stop talking. His skin was pale and sweat beaded on his brow as I buckled him.

"Linda, you drive. I will stay with him." I was hoping to reassure him by sitting with him, but as I got into the car, he lost consciousness.

CHAPTER 11

*A*s we made our way to the house, I couldn't stop holding Sinn's hand in the backseat. I glanced at the shops in Drima Falls and prayed Sinn hadn't sacrificed his life for us. His wounds continued to leak dark fluid, staining his shirt and he was still coughing up blood. His skin was clammy to the touch, and his color continued to fade. While I was still reeling from the encounter with that Gracko he was getting weaker. We would have died, but Sinn saved us. Just as he had been doing since I summoned him. Were demons always so selfless?

Linda was driving above the speed limit, but I wasn't concerned about another ticket. The only thing on my mind was getting Sinn home and finding a way to heal him.

"We're here," Linda said as she parked the car in front of the house and rushed around to help me move Sinn inside.

Sinn moaned in pain as we pulled him from the car. "I think his shoulder is dislocated," I said.

We stumbled several times, supporting his weight as we made our way to the door. By the time we got inside, Sinn had passed out again from the pain. I had never seen him so weak and in so much pain. Blood dripped from his chin to his chest, and my stomach rolled. Ravana was going to pay for this. First, she hurt my daughter, and now, Sinn.

"Let's take him to your room," Linda suggested, and we headed in the direction of the stairs. "It will be easier for him to rest after I heal him as much as possible. I want to make sure there is no venom in his system," she said in a hushed tone. I hadn't even considered the spider was poisonous and my heart squeezed.

After five minutes of struggling to get him up the stairs, we finally got Sinn to my room and laid him carefully on the bed. I removed his shirt so Linda could get a better look at his wounds. The bruising didn't look as bad, but the wounds looked infected with the surrounding skin, red and puffy.

"Linda, can you heal him now?" I asked.

Linda didn't hesitate and knelt on the floor beside the bed with her hands on Sinn's chest. She closed her eyes and a white ball of energy emerged from her fingertips. She had to use a powerful healing spell due to how serious Sinn's injuries were. A wave of energy spread through the room as Linda chanted the spell and moved her hand over Sinn's body. The air rippled in waves like heat from the pavement on a hot summer day.

She started at his head. The white ball lit up Sinn's body as she moved down his body. His body jerked as the energy infused his flesh and the tissue began to heal. The slices in his skin closed as the bruising faded away.

When he groaned, I put my hand in his and squeezed to let him know I was there. Linda's spell was working, quickly. His injuries faded away and his body stilled. His breathing calmed, and I assumed the worst was over.

Linda finished the spell, and the white energy disappeared

from her hand. Sinn's body was still, but he looked peaceful, as if he was having a nap.

I hugged my friend tight. "Thank you for saving him, Linda. I don't know what I would have done without you."

Linda laughed. "You may have turned him into a toad, or a mouse." I laughed with her, knowing it was true. My magic was a shit show.

"Why is he still unconscious?" I asked, with my eyes roaming over his sexy, but still form.

"He was hurt bad, Bree. My magic has closed his wounds and leeched the venom from his blood, but his body still needs to recuperate. He needs to rest," she said.

"We should leave him to it then," I replied, and we both left my room, closing the door behind us.

I kept checking on Sinn from time to time to make sure he was okay while Linda went home to rest and change her clothes. I didn't trust that the Dark God or Ravana not to retaliate against Sinn and kill him while he was vulnerable. The next time I went into my room, Sinn was sitting up, propped against my pillows.

I rushed to his side. "You still need to rest, Sinn."

"What I need to do is bathe," he said with a weak smile. He was better, but he lacked his former vitality. His voice held a crackle that concerned me, but I recalled Linda's words. He needed to rest.

"Okay, let's get you to the tub," I said and helped him into the bathroom. I helped him out of his clothes and got him situated in the bathtub before turning on the tap. Steam rose from the water when I was about to leave the room but he grabbed my wrist.

"Stay with me. There is room in here for both of us. The water will relax you, too."

My cheeks warmed. He had seen me naked before so it

shouldn't be a big deal, but I had never bathed with anyone except Marcellus. Still, he had almost died to save me, and if I was honest, I wanted to stay with him. I nodded and took my clothes off.

Sinn still seemed too weak to do anything, so I helped him clean the dried blood from his skin. Focusing on him made me forget the embarrassment of being naked with him in the tub.

Once we were both clean, we lay in the tub and he massaged my shoulders as I leaned against his chest. I moaned as his fingers did their magic and was disappointed when he was ready to get out. He brushed his teeth, and I helped him back into my room and lay him on the bed. "You know how I need to get my strength back. I need you."

How could I have forgotten? He was an incubus demon, and they needed sex to feed. My mind went back to Linda's comment as we were bringing Sinn up the stairs and her hasty departure. I groaned. Linda knew we would have sex.

I nodded at Sinn as I removed my towel. My hair still dripped to the carpet and ran in rivets between my breasts. I had to help him and I had been thinking about the last time we were together. It was perfect.

Sinn moved his hand to my waist and kissed the side of my temple, trailing his hand down my wet body to my thighs and back up. Each light caress sent a firestorm racing through my blood.

"Let's get you dry first." He picked up my towel and gently cleaned my body with it. It was sensual, the way he moved the cloth over my skin and I closed my eyes, enjoying the sensation. Sinn had a way of making me feel beautiful. Worshipped.

My eyes jerked open when I felt his hot breath fanning my exposed nipple. He was staring up at me as he blew air on my heated flesh, but continued his ministrations with the towel. The way he looked up at me, made me feel like a goddess.

My legs became shaky as Sinn's tongue darted out to caress the hardened peaks. He added slight pressure, flicking harder as his hands roamed my body. The towel fell forgotten to the floor.

When he noticed me sway on my feet, struggling to support my weight under the sensations racking my body, he took my hand and led me to the bed. He laid me on the bed, his naked body settled over me as his mouth claimed mine in a searing kiss. Part of me wanted to be gentle, trying to remember he was recovering from an injury, but as his hands clutched my body, I could find no evidence of his weakness.

I pressed my lips to his with renewed fervor, dominating the kiss. I wanted this man, and not because I needed to help him recharge. Every cell in my body yearned for him. He was fast becoming an addiction I was loath to break.

I rolled us over, still kissing him, and his hands came up to my bare waist as I straddled him on the bed. The heat of our skin moving against one another warped through my body and made me tingle everywhere. A cascade of awareness washed over me. Every nerve ending seeking the addiction known as Sinn. I moaned as I moved over him, taking his thick erection inside me.

With a firm grip on my waist, Sinn began to rock me on top of him. As I ground against his straining cock, his hands reached up to cup my breasts and he squeezed gently. He rolled my nipples between his thumb and forefinger. I threw my head back as a series of moans escaped my lips.

I was still moving against him when my core began to tighten. I rocked faster, thrusting down on him. Sinn felt my body stiffen against his and rolled me back onto the bed.

"Not so fast, Bree," he said with staggered breath.

Sinn hovered over my body and kissed me, his tongue exploring my mouth while his hands moved lower and lower. I gasped into his mouth as his hand found my core and teased my engorged clit. His fingers stroked and glided across my opening without touching me where I needed him to.

When I was seconds from release he stopped, but before I could complain, a finger eased in, filling me, and I arched my back off the bed from the sensation. His mouth moved from my lips to my chest and I became a slave to his hands and magical mouth. My moans encouraged him, and he trailed kisses lower until I could feel his breath against the apex of my thighs.

Bracing myself for the feel of his tongue on me, I fisted my hands in his hair and tugged, eliciting a groan from his wicked lips just before he latched them on my sensitive flesh.

"Oh, God!" I yelled, barely able to breathe through the sensations racking my body. His tongue was even more talented than the last time, and I teetered on the cusp of an orgasm while he kept me perched on the apex.

I wasn't going to last long if he kept this up. His tongue felt like heaven and I kept moving my hips up to get more of it. When my body stiffened and shuddered as I fell over the edge screaming his name. Sinn did not stop licking and sucking as I rode out my climax.

With glistening lips, he came back up. "I love tasting you."

I could barely nod as my legs still felt shaky and I couldn't move. His lips touched mine, and I could taste myself on him. A sensual seduction only Sinn could create.

I was breathless while his mouth moved on mine but I didn't need air. I needed him. Sinn may need to recharge, but he still put me first, and that was so hot.

He positioned himself at my entrance without breaking the kiss, and in one swift motion, we were one. He thrust slowly into me, filling me to the hilt before moving back out and slamming home. I tried to thrust back to increase the tempo, but he seemed intent on torturing me by not moving faster. He continued with that motion, moving his hips while he thrust into me until I couldn't take his teasing anymore.

I wrapped my legs around him and pulled him deeper, moaning louder at the deep angle. He sped up and gripped my waist, increasing his speed. Our moans filled my bedroom, but I sought more of the erotic pleasure surging through my body.

I tried to keep my eyes open so I could stare at the beautiful demigod and incubus demon that was in my bed, pleasing me but as I neared another orgasm, I didn't want the sensations to end.

"Let me get on top," I said, and Sinn smirked at me through hooded eyes.

"As you wish, your highness."

I didn't need any more encouragement. As he laid his back on the bed, I straddled him and he pushed inside me, making me throw my head back. Without allowing me to recover, Sinn lifted his hips and continued thrusting upward. My moans had turned into screams and I grabbed the edge of the headboard while he ravaged me, but it did nothing to stay the building fire inside me.

Sinn slowed down and allowed me to take the lead. His hands grabbed my ass and he shut his eyes while I moved my hips in torturous circles. I leaned down to kiss him while he continued moving inside me.

His mouth moved to my neck, nibbling gently as he pushed into me. My hands gripped his shoulders, and I felt him thicken inside me. His girth stretched me to the point of pain, sending us both over the edge. My eyes rolled to the back of my head as I tried to get my breathing under control.

Sinn brushed my hair away from my face. The sweat stuck to my skin and I loved it.

"What would I do without you?" he asked in a quiet voice.

I winked at him. "Let's not find out. You should be glad you have me," I said breathlessly.

We rolled onto our backs before Sinn pulled me closer and kissed my forehead.

"Do you want to go again?"

I laughed at the delight in his eyes. "I see you've gotten your strength back."

He answered by crawling on top of me. I could feel his erection against my thigh.

"Let me show you," he said.

<h1 style="text-align:center">CHAPTER 12</h1>

The next morning was different from the last time Sinn shared a bed with me. I woke up feeling refreshed and for the first time, I wasn't feeling guilty that I had been with him. The prior day's events replayed over in my mind. Marcellus' kind face remained with me, but I wasn't feeling like I had betrayed him and I hoped I was on the road to accepting that he would want me to be happy.

I turned to my side, clutching the sheet to my chest as my eyes roamed over Sinn. I examined his well-built body and admitted that I wanted him. To feel his lips on mine, his taut muscles as he held me. Get a grip, girl, I thought and looked away as he slept soundly. The warning from Elder Sabrina replayed in my head and I wondered what Sinn's goals were. For weeks now, we followed the leads to save my daughter. But, not once did the conversation of his future come up. I wished that I was telepathic or could tell if his feelings for me were real. He needed me for sex and he seemed to care but that could be our summoning bond. Why was I so worried about his plans? There was no future for us.

I lay in bed, listening to Sinn's strong even breaths. Two

sexual encounters weren't enough to give him my heart. I remembered how he fought to save my life in several situations. Wasn't that enough to trust him? But what if trusting him was what he wanted all along? He was also infected and cursed by the Dark God. Without a cure, he was weakened. His primary goal could be to save himself.

I kicked my legs restlessly in bed, trying to purge my tumultuous thoughts. He had every right to try to cure himself and had done nothing but protect me and help me. Sabrina's warning was hard to shake off, and I dragged my body out of bed.

Perhaps, focusing on something else would help. I slipped into a large sweatshirt and slouch socks before I strolled from the bedroom. Sinn still needed rest to recover, and I didn't want to be the reason he woke up early when his body should be healing.

I stood in the hallway for a moment, looking left then right. Linda had returned and was staying in the guest room, although I doubted, she was still sleeping since she was always awake before dawn. I made my way to Chloe's room and peaked in, wishing she would wake and smile at me, telling me she was fine and start the pancakes. I missed our Saturday morning breakfast ritual. I cursed the witch who had betrayed my daughter's trust.

My mind drifted to Ravana Victious and how she had trapped us in her home. There had been no news about her and the events that unfolded in her house meant she knew we had discovered her duplicity and we would be walking into another trap if we tried a location spell again.

I sighed as I moved to the foot of Chloe's bed. I sat at the end and touched her arm. It was cold. Like it had been when she played outside in the fall and forgot to put on a jacket. Kids had a knack for ignoring the elements. Every minute with my daughter had been a blessing, and I wondered how long I had left before I lost her.

"You shouldn't beat yourself up. She isn't going to die before we find a solution," Linda said as she stood by the door, leaning against the doorjamb, with a coffee in her hand. I didn't hear her approach, but her presence made me feel better.

I patted Chloe's arm, telling her without words I would be here for her until she took her last breath. In my heart, I wished we could switch places, and I was the one cursed instead of her. But, even the Dark God didn't curse a witch with faulty magic.

Linda seemed to read my mind when she said, "I remembered we talked about fixing you up before everything went south."

"You say fix me up like I'm some kind of broken machine. I doubt it's that simple."

"Well… no offence, but machines can break and need fixing. You are also in need of repair we just need to figure out what caused your magic to malfunction."

It was ironic that I wanted my mind off Sinn and our relationship only to have Linda suggest we look for the root of my magic issues. Wasn't there a saying about being careful what you wished for?

"I don't think I can go now. Besides, the way you said it on the way back from the coven retreat, it was pretty obvious that the person you want me to consult with, isn't in Drima Falls. I don't think this is the right time to go looking for a magic healer when we need to find Ravana Victious. Chloe has to come first," I said and Linda sighed.

"I'm not going to argue whether we should fix your magic now or later. And I admit that we need to find Ravana.

She is the only link to the Dark God and our best chance at ending all this."

"Fixing my magic could turn into a wild goose chase. We don't have time for that. Let's focus on finding Ravana."

Sinn walked into the room wearing just his pants, and I swallowed hard. I was still awestruck by his physique, though he didn't seem to notice he looked like a Greek god. He pointed towards the door. "I think there is someone in the living room," he said and I wondered who entered without knocking.

"Who has a key to the door?" Linda asked and when I shook my head to indicate no one, we both knew what awaited us. No human could enter my house unnoticed and that meant that a witch was sitting in my living room. Could it be Ravana Victious? I wondered as I rushed out of the bedroom and towards the carpeted steps.

Getting to the living room, I paused when my eyes met those of Elder Sabrina's and she wasn't smiling. I shuffled closer to her and my mind raced as I wondered why she was sitting in my living room.

"Elder Sabrina, what an honor," I said with a smile that she didn't return. She stood up and looked me over from head to toe. Her eyes shifted to Linda and Sinn and a frown formed on her face.

"I wish I was here on a courtesy visit. But, I am afraid that this is a summons that you are all to appear before the coven council at dusk."

"Why?" Linda asked, taking a few steps forward, her eyes afire with curiosity and fear.

"Why does the council want to see us? We have no business with them," I said.

Elder Sabrina looked at us for a moment before laughing loudly. "You forget who you are talking to. Think carefully about the summons and come prepared to defend yourself. I must tell you that I asked to deliver this message myself because I believe you are good witches and there is still a chance to save you. But actions have consequences and in the last few weeks, you have strayed from our teachings," she said. This wasn't good for us. This wasn't good for Sinn.

"What are the odds that we would find favor in their sight?" I asked as Elder Sabrina turned to leave and she paused. Then, she turned to face me and a wicked smile formed to the side of her mouth.

"You never can tell. Remember, you must appear before the council at dusk. Don't forget. There will be grave consequences for non-appearance."

Before I could say anything else, Elder Sabrina disappeared.

"Am I the only one that thinks Elder Sabrina was kind of hostile toward us?" Linda asked.

"I didn't like her scary smile, but I don't count her as hostile because she had tried to save Chloe."

I turned to face Sinn, as he crossed his arms, looking at me sternly.

"She has always been hostile to me. So, I don't get why you think she wouldn't be hostile today. If I weren't here, she would have been friendlier. But, enough about her attitude. I don't care how she talked to us, I care what she said. You have been summoned and as much as the coven hates incubus demons, I must appear before them. How do we overcome this hurdle?"

"Well, I'm going to assume that we are being summoned because of the use of dark magic. We can assume, we won't be let off the hook. They will insist on prosecuting someone," Linda said, and I knew she was right. The council would want to make an example of one of us or all of us. Sinn was the perfect scapegoat for them. And judging by Sabrina's hatred from him, she would encourage Sinn's prosecution.

I shook my head and faced Linda. "Why don't we run? Avoid the witches that want to judge our life choices?"

"Are you serious right now? We are talking about elder witches here. They can find us wherever we run. Even if we move out of the country or fly to Africa, they would find us. We couldn't find Ravana Victious with our magic and you think we stand a chance against the twelve elders of the witch coven? Let's be realistic!"

"What would you have me do then? We can't appear before them. Sinn will be used as a scapegoat because his kind has laid a bad precedent for him. Are you suggesting we walk him to his death?" I asked and Linda was quiet for a moment. She glanced between me and Sinn and it was obvious that there was nothing she could say to the contrary.

"We can't leave Drima Falls. This is the only place with information on how to defeat the Dark God and save Chloe. It would be foolish to leave," Sinn said.

"But you can't come with us to the council," I snapped back.

"We have to appear before them and state our case. If I'm sent back to the demon world, you can always bring me back here," he said in a low voice.

"Are you forgetting the fact that I brought you into the human world by mistake? I don't think I can summon you again. At least, not without breaking the world in half. Plus, the Book of Lost Shadows shouldn't be used too frequently. The power can get intoxicating. I don't want to risk becoming addicted to it. We need to find a solution if we can't run, and we can't fight the twelve elders. They would end us without hesitation."

With this, I sat down and looked at them. The heavenly

feeling, I had woken up to had been replaced by fear and anger. Although nobody said it, we were helpless, at the mercy of the council. We didn't have time for their trial and we couldn't avoid it.

"We have to attend. Take our chances against the council. If it turns out that they aren't on our side, or they are biased, then we would fight our way out of there or die trying," Sinn said.

I hoped he didn't mean the part about dying at the council meeting. It was obvious that we had to face the council. What were the chances for two witches and an incubus demon hated by all other witches? The fact that Elder Sabrina was in the council and would be obligated to testify against us made my heart beat faster. Using the Book of Lost Shadows was a mistake, and I hoped it wouldn't cost us our lives.

CHAPTER 13

The invitation came later in the day. I was still skeptical as I opened the letter sealed with the blood of the eldest witch in the council. This was the first time I was abruptly summoned, but it wasn't the first time I heard about this kind of practice. I opened the letter, and Linda and Sinn moved to my side. The address disappeared immediately, I glanced at Linda.

"What was that?" Sinn asked, and my shoulders sagged. The letter dissolved into ashes, and I dusted my hands and matched Sinn's gaze.

"That was the official invitation by the council. It is a view once kind of letter. When I opened it, I saw the location for the meeting," I said. The pensive look on their faces indicated they wanted more information.

"Well, the meeting place is one we have been to before. It's after the bridge at the border of Drima Falls," I said, and Linda frowned.

"The initiation woods?" she asked, and I nodded.

"That is the area where we went to find the elder tree for the first potion for Chloe. I know going there won't bring any fond memories. I hope I don't act out against the council," I said, and Linda's eyes widened.

"You can't act in anger against the elders. Ravana would love to see you oppose the council and it would give her a reason to kill you. Do you want to be at her mercy?" Linda asked.

"Of course not. I know she would jump at the chance to kill me. She has never liked me. Maybe she chose Chloe because she hates me so much, but I will be standing in front of a council where she's an elder and she will work against us. She would be foolish to attack us when there are several other witches almost as powerful as she is. We should be physically safe while in the council's presence," I said, still fearing something could go wrong.

"We leave in an hour. You don't want to be late before the council," I said and walked to the kitchen as my stomach growled. I grabbed a mug from the cupboard and poured myself another cup of coffee. The smell had been luring me since I finished the last one.

"Why are you guys scared of your leaders? What's the essence of leadership if the followers fear the leaders more than they respect them?" Sinn asked, and I took a sip of my coffee before I turned to him. The fiery liquid scalded my throat, and didn't calm my nerves. He was right. I was scared of the council. But there was a valid reason for my fear.

I put a piece of bread in the toaster. "My use of the Book of Shadows is against our laws. The council has no tolerance for the use of dark magic. I need to have a valid defense for my actions. Trying to save my daughter is not a sufficient excuse. I don't know…" I waited in silence for the toaster to pop, then grabbed the butter before spreading it on the warm bread as Sinn stepped closer to me.

"I know we won't die today. I also know you won't suffer

any punishment from the council, either. I would die before I let anything happen to you," Sinn said, and I prayed he didn't mean that literally. He didn't understand that if he tried to stop a death sentence on me, it would only delay the conviction. We would be tried for our crimes against the council, and our punishment could be more severe due to Sinn's heroism.

"I will do the talking. Please stay quiet and reduce your replies to one-word answers and be as brief as possible if you are asked multiple questions," I said and Sinn nodded. I hoped he listened to me as I tried to imagine the kind of punishment we would receive for our transgressions. I put my toast on a plate when I realized that I had lost my appetite.

An hour later, I eased the car out of the driveway and exited the gates of my property. As we passed through the main street, shops closed and workers waved goodbye to their employers. Small towns seemed to operate on the same schedule, with evenings saved for family dinners and evening events. For several minutes, we said nothing, and the silence gave me a moment of self-reflection. I glanced at Sinn in the back seat using the rear-view mirror, then at Linda and I wondered what was on their minds. The silence was oppressive, but I couldn't blame them.

We couldn't fight our way out of this, so diplomacy was our only option. My mind drifted to stories of people who had visited the council and had tried to fight their way out of a guilty verdict. They all ended up in the Underworld, even for crimes not as nefarious as the use of dark magic. I sighed and faced the road as we neared the bridge. It was not going to be easy, but there must be a way to win over the council without dying. If not for myself, for Linda. Everything she had done had been for me and Chloe. She didn't deserve to be here.

I swerved onto the dirt road that led to the gateway into the woods. The branches swayed in the trees, giving the impression they waved our last goodbye. Soon, we came to the sign of the witch coven, carved into the tree. A sign only Linda and I could see. An ominous reminder of the laws we had broken. I parked the car and unlocked the doors. "This is it," I said, ending the awkward silence that had suffocated us on the ride over.

Sinn unbuckled his seatbelt. "What do we do if Ravana is on that council? She can't be allowed to leave alive. But, you said we can't fight the council. It could be viewed as an act of war. What do you do when your enemy is a council member?" Sinn asked.

I wanted to reassure him, but to my knowledge, this had never happened before. "I don't know. Let's hope she is still MIA."

Sinn frowned. "And if she is there? We can't accuse her of being a traitor without evidence. It's your word against hers. What will you do, Bree?" Sinn asked, and I took a deep breath. I tried not to think about what would happen if I saw Ravana. Would I kill her? Would I control myself? Could I, knowing what she did to Chloe? I had no idea. But, I knew I had to find a way.

"I don't know. Accusing her would put us in a precarious position. I hate to admit it, but if Ravana is here, we must respect the council and keep our grievances with her to ourselves until we can prove her traitorous actions," I said, getting out of the car. Sinn and Linda followed me and we walked past the marked tree. It took us fifteen minutes to arrive at the area reserved for the council.

The cottage looked rustic, but was reinforced by magic.

The sturdy log walls contained an arced table where the elders held their meetings and their trials. As we approached the council of the twelve most powerful women in the witch coven, a chilling sensation surrounded me.

"It is nice of you to join us, Breena," Elder Medithe, the oldest eldest witch in the coven and the most powerful, said, and we moved to the middle of the room.

I looked around and counted the elders present. Instead of twelve, there were eleven, and I wasn't surprised when Ravana was absent. I looked at Elder Medithe, Elder Yuri, Elder Indira, Elder Eliphas, Elder Levyn, Elder Gwydon, Elder Catherina, Elder Prospero, Elder Litara, Elder Varma, and Elder Sabrina. Seeing Elder Sabrina gave me a sense of reassurance and I bowed softly, looking at Sinn and Linda as they did the same.

"My Elders, when the council calls, it is an honor to answer. Will you tell me why we were summoned to you this evening?"

I glanced at Elder Medithe, and she was looking to her fellow elders. Immediately, I followed her gaze and realized her eyes were fixed on Sinn. Surely, this wasn't about him.

"Distinguished members of this sacred council, it is clear and seen by our own eyes that Breena and Linda have committed an offense. Shall I commence sentencing?" she said,

I looked around and matched Elder Sabrina's gaze, but she looked away. It was obvious that we were on our own and I turned back to Elder Medithe. "You want to sentence us already?" I asked, and she shot me a deadly look.

"No one gave you the right to speak," Elder Varma replied in a thick accent, and I scoffed. If we were going to go down without being heard, then there was no reason to respect the laws of the coven.

I took a deep breath and looked at Elder Medithe, who was watching me like a tiger tailing its prey. "Why would you sentence us without giving us a chance to defend ourselves? What's the point of appearing before you if all you want to do is sentence us unjustly?"

"You call this unjust? How dare you? We have been lenient enough!" Elder Sabrina said, and the vehemence in her voice shocked me. I stared at her for a second, speechless and wondering about her sudden hostility. Then, Elder Medithe's voice jerked me back to reality.

"If we give you a chance to speak before us? What would you want to say? What defense have you got for your actions?" she asked.

"Defense or not, you need to give us a chance to be heard," I said confidently and matched the gaze of the most powerful witch in the coven. One that could kill me with a flick of her hand.

"Alright. Speak!" Elder Medithe said, and several elders turned to face her.

"It is clear that they disobeyed the orders of the coven. Why are we wasting time?" Elder Sabrina said, and I glanced at Linda and Sinn. I couldn't believe she had turned on us, and I wondered what Elder Medithe would do.

"Are you suggesting the council is a waste of time? They want to defend themselves. We have to give them an opportunity. Anyone who isn't in support can leave," she said and I sighed in relief, looking around as the ten remaining elders kept quiet.

"Speak," Elder Medithe said, and I knew I had to choose my words carefully.

"Thank you for this opportunity. I know you view us as guilty and are eager to sentence us. Before you make examples of us, you should know there is a valid reason for our actions. After the coven retreat, I got home and found that my daughter had been cursed. She had a dark energy surrounding her," I said, and the elders began to murmur. "Yes, I was as shocked as you are. Dark magic is forbidden among witches, and this means that someone is practicing dark spells. As a mother, I panicked, wanting to do anything to help my daughter. She was on the verge of death, and I chose a course of action I would never consider under normal circumstances. I was desperate, and since dark magic was used to curse my daughter, it was obvious that dark magic must be the solution."

"Why didn't you come before the council? Why didn't you come to us to help?" Elder Medithe said.

"I was out of my mind with grief and did the first thing that came to mind. It was the wrong decision, but time was of the essence and I needed to act fast. I used dark magic. I knew it was forbidden. But I was desperate. I knew my magic was faulty, but I used it anyway. The result of my first magical attempt was Sinn," I said, and pointed at him. The way they all looked at him indicated that they couldn't wait to get their hands on him and punish him for appearing before them. I hoped I was convincing enough.

"You summoned an abomination," Elder Sabrina said.

"He isn't an abomination," I snapped back. "At first, I thought him to be a mistake, but later, I realized that he was a blessing in disguise. Yes, he is an incubus demon and we have a bad history with his species. But, calling everyone we meet bad and an abomination isn't fair. How would we feel if humans called every witch bad? Since I summoned him, all he has done is protect me. He has saved my life countless times, as well as Chloe's. In the last two months, I've realized that we are all in danger. The world as we know it is ending and soon, dark forces will rule. There are enemies within our ranks and my daughter is just the first of many casualties," I said, and Elder Medithe frowned.

"What do you mean?" she asked, but as I tried to talk, I felt the presence of dark magic, and I faced Elder Medithe. She stood from the table with her eyes glued on an empty spot in the room. She felt it, too. Then a whirlwind appeared.

CHAPTER 14

The council elders shielded their eyes against the leaves and twigs that were being carried in from the forest. Someone was entering the sacred council with dark magic. I couldn't believe the audacity of such an action. This was the most powerful collection of witches on earth. I craned my neck to see who dared to interrupt the council elder's meeting in such a way. The wind subsided and the form of a person emerged from the whirlwind.

By the time the leaves and twigs had settled on the floor and everybody had taken their seats, Ravana Victious stepped out from the chaos and looked as beautiful as ever. While, dark, and imposing, her black dress was perfectly fitted to her curvaceous body and had a train that was following her, sweeping the floor. Her hair was now long and a silky chestnut color that accented her now creamy skin. She looked like she was in her twenties again.

She smirked at me, mocking me for my failure, and I had to pull my hands into fists to stop myself from attacking her. Sinn grabbed my hand in his and he squeezed gently, his way of reassuring me that he was on my side. There was no point in getting angry; Ravana had transcended the need for secrecy. Her power rolled off her in waves, and for the first time, I feared for the council.

I relaxed into Sinn's touch, grateful that he was with me. I was still wary of the council elders, though. I knew they didn't like or trust Sinn, but I wasn't going to let them harm him, incubus demon or not. It didn't matter that my magic was off, I would protect Sinn with my life as he had protected me.

Ravana was still showing off. The clouds were even darker than they should be and crackled with lighting. She smiled snidely as she controlled the elements and made the council members whisper.

As she walked to stand in front of the council table, the clouds cleared and the evidence of brimming nightfall was revealed in the sky.

Twenty-two pairs of eyes fixed on her, and none were happy. The elders looked dumbstruck at Ravana's 'grand' entrance, shooting her vehement looks. She appeared to enjoy the attention, walking slowly and deliberately like she was a bride on her wedding day.

No witch would dare try what Ravana had. The few witches who ever practiced dark magic did it cowering and with fear, in the safety of their homes or in secluded places where the council elders would not be able to detect any disturbance. Everyone knew the consequences of using dark magic in Drima Falls. She had abandoned all pretense of working in the shadows.

Ravana's little stunt was evidence that she no longer cared to hide the fact that she was using dark magic, and that meant she was more powerful than we thought. The Dark God had empowered Ravana, and she was proud of it.

"Ravana, nice of you to join us," one of the elders, Yuri, said, with obvious sarcasm.

"I'm here now. I had some things to attend to," Ravana said, sounding bored like she had better things to do than gracing the council elders with her presence. She swept her eyes across Linda, Sinn, and I and we all stared at her in shock. There was something in her eyes, like annoyance and contempt. She hated us, perhaps because we escaped from her house the other day. Still, her anger didn't rival mine.

"Don't let her anger you. She wants us to react, so don't give her what she wants," Linda whispered to me when she noticed the murderous look in my eyes.

I nodded at her, knowing she was right. But that didn't mean I didn't want to walk up to Ravana and scratch her eyes out. Maybe choking her till she was purple in the face would appease my anger, but I doubted it. She was a monster. I trusted her with Chloe, and she repaid me by bringing her to the brink of death. Despite Linda's warning, I knew I would have attacked her if I had a chance of defeating her. Hell! All three of us were no match for the Dark God, or Ravana.

While we were unable to defeat Ravana, that didn't mean no one else could. Powerful council members could be killed by other powerful council members. I glanced up at the elders at their table. All twelve were now in attendance, though Ravan stood close to me with her sneer in place.

Even if Ravana had powers from the Dark God, eleven council elders should be enough to put her down or capture her. I smiled with the knowledge that we could defeat Ravana if we had the other witches on our side. Judging by the council table, it looked like we could have all of them. The only thing Drima Falls witches hate more than incubus demons was dark magic.

"How could you, Ravana? Why would you walk into a

council meeting with a dark magic fanfare? You dare to desecrate the seat of the council elders by bringing dark magic to our sacred domain?" Ravana's eyes snapped to Medithe, the elder witch in the council, but she made no reaction or indication that she heard her.

Medithe slammed a fist on the table. "You should be eviscerated on the spot for that act alone. Have you no respect for the ancient code of the witches? Have you no reverence left for our ancestors that have sat in this council for centuries?" Medithe wasn't backing down. Ravana's lack of response fueled her anger.

The other elders allowed Medithe to talk to Ravana while they watched with anger in their eyes. It was unheard of.

Everyone's eyes widened when Ravana let out a loud, mocking cackle. She laughed with contempt and hatred. The malevolent sound held the undertone of evil, and I shivered as she continued her rude response.

She looked the council elders in the eye. "You want to eviscerate me? Go on. Try it. You will find that you are no match for me. I should warn you that my power is far greater than you think. Anyone who attacks me will die."

Indira stood up. "Enough of this disrespect, Ravana. We will not sit here and listen while you make a mockery of us and our ancestors."

Ravana laughed louder. She spread her arms wide, in an inviting manner. "Then punish me. I have broken the code of the witches. I proudly use dark magic and will again. I am the messenger of my god."

Medithe spoke this time. "Gwydon, Catherina and Varma, restrain Ravana. She seems to have forgotten the power of the council. She may be the Dark God's minion, but she is but one witch."

Gwydon, Catherina, and Varma stood up, intending to

attack Ravana and restrain her, but she shot out webs from her hands, suspending them to the wall behind the table.

Linda's eyes bulged out. "Ravana has gone mad. She has completely overstepped the council's rules. How could she be so blatantly oppositional? They will never let her live."

Sinn kept looking intently at Ravana like he should do something, but he didn't want to give the elders a reason to turn on him if anything went wrong.

Medithe released the elders with her power. "One witch against eleven? Ravana, I think you should rethink the odds and surrender quietly."

Ravana's smile was murderous. She was enjoying this game. "And who told you I was alone?"

Medithe's eyes widened at the possibility that there were more traitors seated in the council. As she looked at her fellow members, elder Sabrina jumped from her seat on the council and joined Ravana.

"You?" It was Eliphas that spoke. "How could you be on the side of evil, Sabrina?"

"It is none of your business what side I am on. I serve myself, and no one else," Sabrina hissed.

"You serve the Dark God, Sabrina. You're not as independent as you think," Litara said in a soft voice that was filled with venom.

"Well, well, well. That's two against ten. The odds are getting better and better." Ravana said as Elder Sabrina tried to kill Eliphas with a death spell. Medithe deflected the spell, and it broke through the wall, hitting a tree in the forest. The bark withered and turned grey as the elm died.

I couldn't believe what was happening. Elder Sabrina was working for the Dark God?

Linda was thinking the same thing because she screamed, "the potion!"

The potion that Elder Sabrina made for us using the ingredients in the forest, at the tree of the old religion, was meant to heal Chloe, but it made her worse. Sabrina had intentionally poisoned Chloe. It was her plan all along to make my daughter worse, and we played into her hands by collecting the ingredients.

I remembered the man that warned me not to give Chloe the potion and how I ignored him. Had he known that Sabrina was a traitor? I wish I had listened.

"You tried to kill my daughter!" I screamed at Sabrina, lunging at her. Sinn held me back. I struggled against his grip, trying to get to Sabrina, but he was unrelenting.

Ravana and Sabrina turned to me. "It was very easy to deceive you. You are too gullible Breena. That's why you're a weak witch and are relying on an incubus demon to fight your battles for you," Sabrina said with a menacing smile.

The elders attempted to spell Ravana and Sabrina while they faced us, but Ravana's reflexes were too quick and she deflected all of them without looking in the elder's direction.

"Breena, you are just too trusting and gullible. A weak witch with nothing left. You're just like your mother," Ravana said.

I was seething with anger, but I stared back at her, calmly. I was not going to take the bait. I tried to think clearly, as I was the least powerful person in the gathering. There was nothing I could do against the combined force of Ravana and Sabrina's dark magic.

"You're both going to pay for putting my daughter in danger. I will make sure of it." I said to Ravana and Sabrina.

Sabrina laughed. "You think this is about your daughter? This is about the Dark God coming back to take over both the human world and the underworld. We are here to ensure his victory. Your daughter is just a pawn in our plan. A mere tool with little importance to the Dark God. We picked sides a long time ago. You have nothing, not even your magic. Not your husband, and certainly not your daughter. You are nothing and I'm going to make sure you die by my hand tonight."

Sinn was holding me against him, fearing I would make a hasty decision and rush at Sabrina or Ravana. "You are wrong. Marcellus may be dead, but that doesn't mean he is not with me. Chloe too. No matter where she is, my baby girl is still with me. But we are not fighting for just my daughter. We are fighting for the whole world. To spare this realm from the Dark God and return him in chains to the underworld."

"Really? You think you can achieve all that? The Dark God is more powerful than you know. Especially since he has weakened the other Gods. No creature is safe from him. He will conquer all." It was Ravana that spoke this time.

"You can try, but the Dark God will not win," I said with confidence.

"And how are you going to stop him? With that faulty magic of yours?" Sabrina smirked. I still gave her no reaction.

"I have my friends with me, and the council elders, too. I am not alone, Sabrina. You are. Why is your Dark God sending you to do his bidding? Why are you doing his dirty work? Sinn and Linda would die for me, but you will die for nothing. If the Dark God wins, he will have no use for you," I said triumphantly.

Sabrina laughed loudly. "The Dark God is executing his plan as we speak. And even if we die, which will not happen, we will be reunited with our master in the underworld. He will reward us for dying for his cause after he conquers the world. You're wasting your time, Breena. You will still die tonight."

Ravana was muttering a spell which Linda tried to disrupt, but Ravana was too powerful. The elders joined forces too to try to stop whatever Ravana was doing, but it wasn't working. She had a dark web of protection surrounding her and their attempts failed.

The elder's power bounced off the dark web and back in their direction. Elder Medithe ducked to miss a ball of energy that bounced off Ravana's protection spell.

"Watch out!" Sinn shouted, and the elders ducked as an invisible blast exploded above their heads. Splinters of wood showered the elders at the table and they would have died if not for Sinn. They looked at him with appreciation in their eyes and renewed respect.

Ravana turned back to the elders with a malicious glint in her eyes. She was done with whatever spell she was conjuring.

"Shall we?" She said as another whirlwind was summoned with the wave of her hand.

Two Grackos emerged from the small tornado. They were even bigger than the one we fought at Ravana's house. A sphinx followed behind them. Its eyes narrowed at me in recognition.

The elders looked stunned at the emergence of the monsters. They had never seen anything like this. They recovered quickly and began to split into groups to fight the three monsters, Sabrina and Ravana. Sinn changed into his demon form, preparing to help us. Linda went and stood with a trio of elders, joining forces to fight in the battle.

I didn't have any reliable powers, but remembered the Stygius blade that I had been carrying since we entered the painting at the Museum of Ancient Arts. I drew it out as the sphinx charged me.

The sphinx lunged at me, but I waited till the last second

before I rolled away and dodged her attack. She was enraged that she had missed me, so I smiled at her, tauntingly.

"We meet again. And you will be defeated again, sphinx," I said.

"I am going to enjoy killing you, and I will not fail this time." She extended her wings and tried to slash me, but I was too fast, and they whirled through empty air.

All around me, the fight with the creatures raged. Ravana had summoned two more Grackos but Medithe was stopping her from summoning more. She held Ravana pinned against a broken wall as she shot a beam of light at her.

Ravana deflected the light and escaped Medithe's grasp, dropping to the floor. She recovered quickly and rolled away from Medithe's attack, stalking toward her. Ravanna's hand formed a ball of black energy as Medithe looked on.

I heard a yelp as Sabrina was being attacked on both sides by Yuri and Indira. They had protection balls surrounding them while they fought Sabrina. She deflected many of their attacks, but several energy balls hit their mark, and it looked like they were winning.

"Stupid, stupid human," the sphinx said as it stalked toward me again.

"I'm not human. I'm a witch," I said as I sliced forward with the Stygius knife and cut her face with it. She hissed her rage and stood on her hind legs, raising her two front legs to stomp on me. I was lucky to escape at the last minute, as Linda sent a freezing spell at the sphinx. I shot her a grateful look as she resumed her battle with one of the Grackos and was glad Sinn was helping her.

The other three Grackos were surrounded by Litara, Gwydon, Catherina, Eliphas, Levyn, Prospero, and Varma. They took on the Grackos two to one and Eliphas was helping with all three, offering assistance to whoever needed it.

"Aim at the mouth!" Linda shouted to the elders, who had no idea how to fight Grackos.

They were frustrated when the Grackos limbs continued to regenerate every time they cut them. I remembered that it was Linda that defeated the Gracko that we fought at Ravana's house with the death spell she shot at its mouth.

The elders took her advice and started to aim their powers at the bellies and mouths of the creatures.

Medithe had dark circles under her eyes and I feared the toll the extended use of magic was having on her. As powerful as the elders were, they were also older women. Ravana had hit Medithe with so much dark energy that she was barely standing. She was bruised and blood dripped from a cut on her arm, but she was still fighting.

The sphinx broke free from the hold that Linda placed on her to discover that I had slashed at her hind legs. When she stepped back, she fell backward, unable to stand on them. As she rolled to her side, I stood over her to taunt her again.

"I thought you were smarter than this, but you always end up on the floor," I said.

She let out a screech and flapped her wings, lifting herself into the air. She turned around and charged at me as fast as she could, with blood dripping down her legs. As she came for me, I braced myself, knowing her weakness was her anger. When I ducked and rolled out of the way she turned, intending to lunge at me again.

I stood and climbed onto the table. It put me at eye level as she approached, screaming her hatred. I jumped as she lunged and collided with the sphinx in midair, then stabbed her eye while holding onto her neck. I jumped down and realized her bloody eye was impaled on my blade, before flicking it to the ground.

While she stumbled around, trying to recover from the pain, I used the table to launch onto her back, then used the Stygius blade to slice through her neck. She screeched as her legs failed her and fell to the floor. She stopped writhing as the blood flowed from the open wound and she fell on her side, as her screams died out. I turned to see who was in need of assistance.

I glanced at Sinn and Linda. They were fighting well together and had killed one Gracko and were turning to another.

I went to help them when tree roots wrapped around my ankles and dragged me to the floor. Elder Sabrina had eviscerated one side of the council hall and the open forest loomed. She was glaring at me in hatred as the roots pulled me outside and suspended me from an ancient tree.

She had injured Yuri, who was crawling on the ground not far from the tree and Indira was on the floor of the chambers, unmoving. Linda and Sinn noticed what was happening, and they charged forward and split up. Linda went to help Medithe, and Sinn ran toward me.

Eliphas and Levyn were also injured, and they lay on the floor moaning. The other elders were still fighting the Grackos, and there were only two uninjured elders left. Sabrina didn't see Sinn coming from behind her, so she wasn't prepared when he threw her down and grabbed her neck with demon hands.

Sabrina struggled against Sinn's hold, and she sputtered as Sinn's claws dug into her. She used a repellant spell to get him off her as Linda blasted the tree roots that were holding me with her power.

I moved to Sinn's side, and we prepared to fight Sabrina together. Her eyes roamed over us with anger and pain. The wound at her neck knit back together as she used dark magic to repair it. "I warned you that you would die by my hand, Breena."

Linda thrust an energy ball at Ravana and she retaliated. I gasped as Linda burst through a chamber wall and rolled onto her back. She stood up, wiping blood from the cut above her eye.

Sabrina charged toward me when I was focused on Linda and shot a dark cloud of energy at me. Sinn moved in front of me and it hit him in the shoulder, sending him backward with the force.

He stumbled and fell to his knees.

"Sinn!" I screamed. "Are you okay?"

"I'm fine," he groaned.

Sabrina rushed toward me, but Sinn stood up and grabbed her again. He held her up by her neck and dug his claws into the soft flesh. I stabbed the Stygius blade into her stomach and Sinn released her. She fell to the floor and spluttered blood.

"It's over, Sabrina," Sinn said to her, with a growl.

"I'm not going to die at your hands, you filthy demon," she said amidst coughing blood.

"Sorry, but you can't always get what you want. In this case, you get me." Sinn smiled, displaying his fangs. He was scary, but not to me. This was Sinn, and I accepted every part of him.

He glanced at me, and I knew what he wanted. "Finish her. She is a disgrace to humanity."

His red eyes returned to Sabrina. "Good thing I never liked you." He extended a claw, then removed Sabrina's head in one swipe. They turned away from her limp body.

Linda was holding up well with Medithe against Ravana and so Sinn went to help with the last two Grackos. He was done with fighting all these monsters and charged at the Gracko closest to him.

With impossible strength, he opened its mouth while Elder Gwydon shot a death spell into its mouth. They killed the last Gracko in no time and before long, only Ravana was remaining.

Several elders went to tend to the injured, and another covered Indira's body with a cloak. The mood was somber, and the battle was not over.

"Stay here," Sinn said to me, and I nodded at him, cupping his face in my hand.

He left me and went to help Linda and Elder Medithe. Medithe was barely hanging on and Sinn took her place in attacking Ravana. He charged at her from behind while she was about to use a spear, she had conjured with dark magic, intending to stab Elder Medithe who had fallen to the floor.

He used a razor-sharp claw to cut Ravana's hand off. It fell with the spear as she shrieked in pain. Sinn lunged at her other hand, but she turned and he cut off her arm at the elbow. It fell beside the hand, still clutching the spear she was going to use to kill Medithe.

"You stupid demon," she hissed angrily. But then she smiled as her arm grew back, like one of the Grackos.

"You're going to wish you had never crossed me," she said as she approached Sinn slowly.

"You think you can kill me?" Sinn laughed as he extended large black wings, flexing them before her as scythes extended from the tips. "You are nothing. I am a demigod and an incubus demon. You're no match for me, Ravana."

"I'm going to send you back to the underworld, along with your little lover and everybody she cares about," Ravana said, and started to shoot her dark magic webs at Sinn.

Sinn blocked her blows and used his wings to throw her

off again. While Ravana was distracted with Sinn, Medithe attempted to get on her feet.

She approached Ravana from behind while she was trying to get a shot at Sinn. Sinn nodded imperceptibly at Medithe just as one of the webs caught him in the ribs and he writhed in agony. It cut through his side and the smell of singed flesh permeated the air.

Elder Medithe wasted no time, and she arced the spear high in the air and brought it down on Ravana's back.

Ravana screamed as the magic in the spear merged with her blood. Black veins marred her skin as the poison moved through her bloodstream. She began to chant, and the black veins slowed their progress.

Sinn groaned from the floor where he had fallen. I rushed to his side and realized that he had returned to human form. That alerted me to the serious nature of his injury.

Before anybody could finish off Ravana, she completed a disappearing spell and vanished into thin air.

I helped Sinn up and Linda quickly supported Medithe before she fell to the floor.

It was over. The creatures and Sabrina were dead, but Ravana escaped within an inch of her life. We all knew that as long as Ravana was alive, the battle wasn't over but for now, we had defeated them. They had time to rest and regroup before she made her next move.

We all gathered under what was left of the council chambers and laid Indira's body on the table.

"We have to arrange for her funeral immediately," Medithe said.

All eyes turned to Sinn.

"We were wrong about you. Perhaps dark magic can be used for good after all. It was unfair to judge you by the transgressions of another. Apparently, we need all the help we can get," Elder Medithe said.

I placed my hand in Sinn's. "He is truly amazing."

Medithe nodded. "You fought valiantly here today, and you saved all of our lives," she continued with a grateful look. She was exhausted though, and I wasn't sure how much longer she could remain on her feet. She turned to me and Linda. "We called you here to judge you, and in turn you saved us. We are humbled by your bravery and your loyalty. We will strive to earn the gift you have given us. I hope you will trust us with your plans, as it seems you have been fighting this war on your own."

I took a deep breath. "Thank you. We will fill you in on everything, but we need some rest."

"Ravana will be back, and we must prepare. Let us heal our wounds today and rest as the coming days will be dark, and not all will survive. We will have to persevere to win this war. The Dark God will not take control of this world. It is our duty to save humanity."

The elders linked their hands together, and a white light formed around them. The light crackled, and they all said a healing spell aloud, chanting it louder and louder.

By the time the light went out, all the elders were whole again, with not so much as a scratch or a bruise.

Medithe put her hands on Linda's forehead and healed her wounds before doing the same for me. I felt invincible as her healing warmth moved through me.

She turned to Sinn. "As a token of my thanks, you are one of us. If you ever need anything, feel free to come to me personally. We will be here for you with open arms."

She tried to heal Sinn, but he was unable to return his skin to its former glory. The smaller bruises faded, but several dark splotches remained. He needed rest, and I feared Ravana's spell did more damage than I realized.

"Thank you once again and I'm sorry I lack the ability to heal you fully," she turned, and together with the other elders, they carried Indira's body from the chambers into the forest. They didn't take the trail that led to the parking area.

"That was unexpected," Linda said and came to help me support Sinn's weight.

I rolled my eyes at her. "That was a disaster. I never want to be in that position again."

"Let's get Sinn home first before you start complaining," Linda said in a teasing tone.

He just laughed and kissed my forehead. "Thank you."

We had almost made it to the Carolla before he groaned and stumbled. We got him to the car, but when we got him situated in the back seat, he was unconscious.

CHAPTER 15

*L*inda and I drove back to my house while Sinn slept in the backseat. We woke him when we returned home, and he stayed awake long enough for us to get him to my bedroom. I figured that he would be hungry by the time he woke up. While I knew his hunger wouldn't be contained to the food variety, I told Linda to go to the kitchen to see if there was something we could cook for him to eat.

"Bree, you had me worried back there," Linda said as we descended the steps to the living room.

"I'm sorry, Linda. I knew what I needed to do, but I understand your fear. I worried about you too. I really don't know what would happen if I lost Sinn, you or Chloe," I replied to Linda.

"Honey, I saw how you cried when he was being beaten. You have feelings for him, don't you?" Linda asked, and winked.

"Oh please. That was just my hormones acting up. I would have cried if you were getting the shit kicked out of you too, so don't read too much into it," I said, turning back toward the steps so I could go check on Chloe.

"Oh yeah? You aren't crying every day because Chloe is still laying on the bed without a cure," Linda added.

I knew that she wasn't going to let the matter drop and whether she was right or wrong, it wasn't something I was ready to discuss with her. I had to do something to stop her teasing me further, so I distracted her.

"Linda sweetie, why don't you head down to the kitchen now," I said, changing the topic.

She understood my cue that I wasn't ready to talk about my personal life. She let it drop, even though I knew she was itching to discuss my future with Sinn. "Sure."

"We could get him some pizza and maybe ice cream," I suggested.

She shook her head at me as she walked to the kitchen, pouting like a child that was being denied her favorite candy.

Linda had every right to be concerned, but I didn't need to think about my feelings for anybody until he was totally healed. I head upstairs intending to check on Chloe and found myself in my room, looking at Sinn. His body was still covered in bruises, and one side of his lips had dried blood on the edge. My heart squeezed as I thought about the position he was put in because he tried to protect Linda and me from Ravana. I had developed an intense hatred for the Dark God and planned retribution, tenfold.

Sinn wasn't supposed to be in pain. He hadn't asked to be summoned. I wished we could exchange bodies, and that I could take away his pain.

He had given us clear instructions not to touch him till he fully woke from his rest, so I decided to leave him to it and check up on my daughter. At least that would keep me busy till he woke up from his sleep.

I walked into Chloe's room to confirm she still lay on the bed looking lifeless. My own daughter had been cursed for weeks and only Linda's magic kept her alive. She infused Chloe with nutrients to sustain her body, but couldn't break the hold the Dark God had on her mind. I wished that I was the one cursed instead. Sometimes it felt like I was. Nobody around me deserved what had happened to them. First, it was Chloe, now Sinn. God only knew who the next person to be hurt because of the Dark God's powers. I wondered why he was so angry at the world.

I put my hand on Chloe's chest to confirm that she was still breathing. "At least she is still alive."

All I wanted was for Chloe to get better. She needed to get better, or I had failed as a parent. I didn't know when the tears began flowing down my face, but I wiped them away as I sat on the bed beside her.

I wished that my magic wasn't faulty. I could have at least protected Sinn and Linda from the monsters that attacked them. Maybe I was cursed and just hadn't reacted like Chloe. Was that possible?

I was smoothing Chloe's covers when I heard a sound at the door. I didn't have to turn around to know it was Linda. She was probably done in the kitchen. I wiped the tears that had streamed down my cheeks, but Linda wasn't one to be deceived. One look at me and she knew I had been crying.

"Hey, are you okay?" Linda asked, putting down the tray of food she had prepared for Sinn so she could give me a quick hug.

"I'm good. I just came in to check on Chloe. I think everything that's happened is catching up to me," I said.

"Don't worry. We'll find a way around it. We will pay a visit to that friend I told you about when we have some time," Linda said, and I nodded.

"What did you make for Sinn?" It smelled amazing, and I hoped she made enough for me.

She showed me the plate of chicken and pasta in primavera sauce with a side of garlic toast. My mouth watered at the scrumptious odor.

"I really hope that your friend will have an answer to my problems," I said to Linda.

"Hey, you don't need to worry, he is the best, "Linda reassured me. As we were talking, we heard Sinn groan from my bedroom.

"Go check on him while I bring out the first aid kit. If he is awake, I want to clean the rest of his wounds," I said to Linda.

"Sinn, what are you doing? You shouldn't try to stand. You aren't strong enough," Linda said in a disapproving tone.

I rushed into the room as she unceremoniously forced him back to bed. She gave me a concerned look, but Sinn didn't see it.

I placed the food on his lap when he was situated in bed. He inhaled the pasta like someone who hadn't eaten for days.

"You were hungry, "I said to him as he gulped down the glass of apple juice Linda supplied with the meal.

"Sorry," he smiled sheepishly, but I was thrilled he was enjoying the food.

"Linda is an amazing cook. I recommend taking advantage while you can."

"Fighting Ravana and Elder Sabrina took a lot out of me. They were stronger than I anticipated," he said.

"Thankfully, you weren't on your own. Everybody worked well together," I said.

I knew that Linda and I fighting Ravana on our own would not have gone well. At least not for us. I was very thankful for Sinn's help.

Sinn was the only one amongst us who had experience fighting these demons. We would have died a long time ago if he hadn't been with us. The elders had realized pretty quickly that we needed him. His expertise as much as his skill.

"I prefer not to be bait for Ravana, next time," Sinn said.

"How are you feeling?" I asked him.

"I'm still in pain, but I will be fine," Sinn said.

Linda took this as a cue to leave the room so I could clean Sinn's wounds comfortably. Elder Medithe already did some of the work in healing him, but something had hindered her power. Linda knew we needed to have our "conversation". She already knew that Sinn and I had slept together twice but we had never spoken about it.

I took the tray from him and placed it on the side table so I could get access to his remaining wounds. He grunted as I put the antiseptic against an open lesion. The fight with Ravana had taken more of a toll on his body than I expected. I continued applying the antiseptic and dressed the rest of the wounds as I recalled when Ravana hit Sinn with her dark magic web. I thought he was going to die right there, and it had been painfully scary.

"I didn't realize demons were such babies," I teased when he grunted again.

"Sucker hurts like hell," he said.

"Honey, I thought you said once you rested, you would be totally healed," I asked.

As I finished cleaning him up, I noticed the bruises that Elder Medithe healed had disappeared completely. While those were less severe, it meant that he would get better in time.

"Most of the injuries are clearing up already. You'd need more rest for the deeper ones to heal over," I said to him pointing to his skin that was turning back to its natural bronze.

"Honey, I'm a demon. You know most wounds won't stay on my body."

We chuckled together, but the sound died out quickly, to be replaced with awkward silence.

"Sinn, we need to talk," I said to him while laying down the tools I used to dress his wounds.

"Yeah, I know, about us, right?" Sinn asked.

We didn't know what to say to each other about our feelings or our last sexual encounter. It was just weird talking to Sinn. He had become a friend as much as a lover. Never in my dreams did I think I would be sitting with one of my closest friends and declaring my feelings for him.

When I first met him, I felt like I was betraying my late husband, but Marcellus has been dead for some time. I didn't need to feel awkward about talking to Sinn. The feelings between us were mutual, that I was sure of.

"You know what, Breena? I admire you. Whatever feelings you have for me I share them. You are an amazing person and mother. I see how you are with Chloe, even though she hasn't moved for weeks. You love Linda more than a sister, and you are mindful of everyone around you. I admire everything about you and I don't regret one moment we had together," Sinn said, pulling me from my thoughts.

"I was just helping you recharge," I teased with a smile.

"We both know it was more than that."

While I knew he cared for me, I wasn't expecting the other things Sinn said to me. It felt good to be appreciated and comforting for him to voice his feelings for me.

"Whew, it sounded like you had that memorized," I said, and released a light chuckle.

"What can I say, the silence was getting awkward. Besides, I have wanted to tell you for some time now," Sinn added.

"Sinn, it's not that I don't have feelings for you. I remember looking at you on several occasions and wondering why you hadn't made a move on me. You are funny, charming, attractive and Lord, you fight well," I said after praying to the Gods in the whole universe to give me courage.

"Still, I am not sure if we should act on our feelings. I'm not positive, but it feels like we don't trust each other enough to enter into anything serious," I said, as I placed my hand in his. He stared at me, and I continued when he didn't respond.

"I mean, you are an incubus demon. I am just a witch. Are we even compatible with each other? Having you with me was the best thing that happened to me since Marcellus died. Don't take this the wrong way, but I don't want to make the wrong decision."

"Honey, you are thinking about this thing too much. Relax. You don't need to remind me that I am an incubus. I know about the history of our species," Sinn teased, easing the tension. "Also, I clearly remember the elders accepting me and approving of me. I understand what you mean though, about you not trusting me, or rather us not fully trusting each other. You are not wrong for being skeptical about your feelings for me. We have time."

I loved how he looked at me while we spoke. It made me feel like I was the only woman in the world. Well, I was the only one in the room at that moment, but I couldn't shake off the feeling that I couldn't trust him. It made no sense since Sinn had helped me countless times. And it wasn't just me. He protected Linda when fighting Ravana, Elder Sabrina, and some of the deadliest demons to enter our world. My lack of faith was annoying and unfair to him.

"I don't want this to spoil our friendship and what we

have, though. I'm flattered that you like me," I replied, and smiled at him.

"Breena, caring for you is easy. We will keep things on the down low for now. I know our enemies could use it against us. Saving Chloe has to be the first priority," Sinn said, placing a light kiss on my forehead.

"Yeah. I agree, and hopefully we will find a way through this," I said.

Having this conversation with Sinn was tough, but I felt better, knowing we were on the same page. His concern for Chloe never ceased to amaze me and made me care for him even more. It made me feel like we could get through anything. I left the room as he started to doze off.

"Hey, how did it go between you guys?" Linda asked as soon as I entered the kitchen. She had a plate of pasta and chicken waiting for me on the table, and I thanked God she was my best friend. I wasn't surprised she knew what was going on upstairs. She knew me better than anyone. She was also a talented witch.

"It went well. Thanks for asking," I said.

"Bree, I left the room, remember? So, I want to know the details of that conversation," she said, crossing her arms.

"Okay, fine. You win. I forget how pushy you are," I said, sounding defeated.

I told her everything I discussed with Sinn over a cup of tea, and she seemed disappointed that we weren't taking our relationship to the next level. Obviously, it wasn't the news she expected to hear.

"What?" I asked her when she scowled at me.

"Nothing. You guys are not dating. Got it," she said, standing up from the chair as if she was about to leave. "By the way, first thing tomorrow we are going to see my friend. We need to do something about your faulty magic and I hope we can sort it quickly," she said as she put on a light jacket.

"You heading home?"

"I want to shower and grab some clean clothes. I will be back in the morning." She winked and left me to eat the amazing meal she had prepared for me.

Even though Linda hadn't said as much, I knew that she was disappointed about the conversation between Sinn and me. It was strange to find she wanted me to move on. Was I holding back? Still, struggling to let go of the past or had Sabrina sabotaged me with her fake fears. Who knew if anything she told us was true? Linda's leaving abruptly was an indication that she was disappointed and didn't want me to know, but she wasn't in a position to decide my future. As much as I loved her, the decision was ours to make. Sinn and I had an understanding I was happy with… for now.

I ate my food in silence, then cleaned the dishes before checking on Chloe and crawling into bed with Sinn. He didn't move and my eyes drooped within minutes of the blankets enveloping me in their warmth. I drifted off with thoughts of the future.

I woke the next morning when my alarm blared. I turned it off quickly, checking on Sinn. He was still asleep, and I decided to leave him to rest. How long had we slept for? It seemed like we had only been in bed for an hour. I showered and went down to the kitchen to make coffee, but Linda was already there. She handed me a full cup.

"You ready to go to Danley?"

"Absolutely," I said, taking a sip.

I left to check on Sinn before we set out. Danley was a

hundred kilometers away from Drima Falls, so we needed to set out early and see the witches overseeing the Falls.

"I need to get to Danley with Linda. Will you be all right on your own?" I asked Sinn as soon as I got into his room.

"Yeah Bree, go and do whatever you need to do. Linda told me that you would need to go to Danley soon. Now is as good a time as any," Sinn said.

I knew that he would be understanding. He was always looking out for me and had been supportive through my anguish over losing my magic. He had hoped that I would get it back.

"Alright, thank you. We promise to be back soon," I said, giving him a reassuring look.

"It's fine. You are the one who needs to be careful. Danley isn't Disneyland. You will have to be careful how you traverse the paths, and most importantly, listen to instructions," Sinn advised.

Ice skittered down my spine as he spoke. He meant no harm and was only advising me about the dangers ahead, but I had never been to the Falls before. How was I supposed to be careful somewhere I'm unfamiliar?

For a minute, I thought of going back on my decision to visit Danley. I had made it this far without magic. Sinn noticed my indecision.

"Hey. I didn't mean to scare you, okay? I'm just warning you. Besides, Linda has been there before, so she will be able to guide you," he reassured me.

We made our goodbyes to Sinn and set out to the Falls. I drove to keep my attention on the road instead of the trials ahead. Drima Falls was a bustle of activity in the morning as patrons grabbed pastries and coffee before starting their daily routines. Once on the highway between Drima Falls and Danley, my mind wandered to what awaited me.

I wondered what it looked like and hoped this visit wouldn't be like the museum or the painting that took us to a magical place. One with an empty town and a bitchy Sphinx.

We arrived in Danley in an hour, thanks to my speedy driving, and I was amazed at how beautiful the place was.

It had a multitude of lavender trees surrounding it and the eclectic array of bushes and colors made it seem like something out of a fairy tale. We had barely gotten past the massive white archway when we noticed a giant shadow standing across from us. I had no idea whose shadow it was or if it was a person at all. I shivered, grabbing Linda's hand, and inclining my head toward it.

"Hey. Don't be scared. That is probably one of the healers we have come to see. He hasn't seen us yet. His body is turned away from us," Linda said, squeezing my hand.

"This place looks so creepy and beautiful at the same time," I said and we both laughed, agreeing it was true.

I shrugged away the creepy sensations emitted by the falls in Danley. We saw a hut as we walked along the path and decided to enter it, hoping we could get some direction.

"Hello," we both said as soon as we knocked on the door and a sickly old woman with white hair exited the house.

I almost screamed when her black eyes narrowed on me but Linda tugged on my arm to prevent my outburst. I tried mumbling my apology, but nothing coherent came out.

"Good morning. Please excuse my friend's reaction. She has never been here before," Linda said, making excuses for me.

"I understand, dear," the old woman said before Linda released my arm.

"Come in," the old woman said, ushering us into her small hut.

It felt like she already knew why we were in Danley, as

she kept casting glances at me and making strange faces. Her behavior was that of one who had condemned us before knowing what we came for.

"Hmmm, I know why you are here. I was warned of your arrival," the old woman said, pulling me from my thoughts.

"You do?" Linda asked.

"Yes. Your friend here has magic that she cannot use," the old woman said.

"How did you know?" I asked, stuttering on my words.

"Dear, this is Danley. The people who visit here are mostly witches, magicians, and those who cast all sorts of spells. They mostly come here for healing. In fact, one of the spirits made it clear to me that we would receive visitors from Drima Falls. When I saw you, I knew that you were the ones she warned about," the old woman said.

"So, what can we do? Is there any remedy to cure her magic? I'm good with spells, and breaking curses. The only curse I can't seem to break is that of the Dark God," Linda said.

I loved how she was ready to help me at any time. Even when I didn't ask it.

"Unfortunately, your friend's magic cannot be returned. She is to stay like this for the rest of her life unless a miracle happens or the Dark God ceases to exist," the old woman explained.

"What do you mean? There has to be a way. That's why we have Danley. You have solutions for every witch's problem here," Linda said as warm tears came rolling down my cheeks.

Danley was our last hope of me getting my magic back, and the last vestige of my world crumbled. How was I going to save Chloe? I couldn't let Sinn and Linda do it alone.

Without my magic, I was just a car without fuel. I was useless.

"I know that is true. If we had a solution or a spell to reverse the effect of this dark magic, I honestly would have given it to you. You know I am telling you the truth."

The old woman looked sorry that she couldn't help me. She shook her head and disappeared into thin air, as I put my hand over my forehead.

"Linda, this can't be it. We have to do something about my magic," I said.

"Yes. But you heard the woman. There is no solution at Danley, so we need to go before we encounter something we are not supposed to. Danley is beautiful and deadly. We have no further reason to be here," Linda said. "But all hope isn't lost. You heard what she said about the Dark God ceasing to exist. We have to get rid of him, and your magic will return." Linda's attempt to make me feel better didn't work.

The drive home was silent. I was too distraught about the news I received in Danley. I knew there had to be a way we could get my magic back, and I wasn't going to give up hope. Even if it meant me meeting the coven members and begging. I was going to do everything it took to get my magic back on track.

I stared at the road as a plan formed. I didn't share it with Linda, as I knew she would hate my idea.

Continue reading the Midlife Curses series, with A Witch in Disguise.

ABOUT THE AUTHOR

Victoria Crawford is a paranormal women's fiction author. She is happily married with three grown children and lives in western Canada with her ever-growing number of cats and two guinea pigs. When she isn't penning stories about magic, demons and other supernatural beings, she is sipping wine, eating chocolate, and plotting her next shenanigan.

Subscribe to Victoria's newsletter at https://www.subscribepage.com/victoria-crawford *for free content and start your journey through Victoria's paranormal world today!*

CONNECT WITH ME!

Website- https://boldbutterflypublishing.com/victoria-crawford/

Booksprout- https://booksprout.co/reviewer/author/view/30781/victoria-crawford

amazon.com/author/victoriacrawford

facebook.com/victoriacrawfordbooks

twitter.com/vcrawfordbooks

goodreads.com/victoria_crawford

bookbub.com/authors/victoria-crawford